PRAISE

MW01616765

"Thor, Baldacci, Flynn, Hamburg. Get ready as Banner fits right in!"

AMAZON REVIEW

"Move over Jack Reacher there's a new guy taking over."

AMAZON REVIEW

"Great stuff. Exciting and fast paced. On par with Flynn & Thor."

AMAZON REVIEW

"The writing was superior, the story line was compelling and the action was top-notch. Sorry I could only give this one a five star rating!"

AMAZON REVIEW

THE DEVIL'S VENGEANCE

A HARRY BAUER THRILLER

BLAKE BANNER

RIGHTHOUSE

Copyright © 2024 by Right House

All rights reserved.

The characters and events portrayed in this ebook are fictitious. Any similarity to real persons, living or dead, is coincidental and not intended by the author.

No part of this book may be reproduced in any form or by any electronic or mechanical means, including information storage and retrieval systems, without written permission from the author, except for the use of brief quotations in a book review.

ISBN-13: 978-1-63696-326-6

ISBN-10: 1-63696-326-9

Cover design by: Damonza

Printed in the United States of America

www.righthouse.com

www.instagram.com/righthousebooks

www.facebook.com/righthousebooks

twitter.com/righthousebooks

HARRY BAUER THRILLER SERIES
Dead of Night (Book 1)
Dying Breath (Book 2)
The Einstaat Brief (Book 3)
Quantum Kill (Book 4)
Immortal Hate (Book 5)
The Silent Blade (Book 6)
LA: Wild Justice (Book 7)
Breath of Hell (Book 8)
Invisible Evil (Book 9)
The Shadow of Ukupacha (Book 10)
Sweet Razor Cut (Book 11)
Blood of the Innocent (Book 12)
Blood on Balthazar (Book 13)
Simple Kill (Book 14)
Riding The Devil (Book 15)
The Unavenged (Book 16)
The Devil's Vengeance (Book 17)
Bloody Retribution (Book 18)
Rogue Kill (Book 19)
Blood for Blood (Book 20)

Lord God, to whom vengeance belongeth; O God, to whom vengeance belongeth, shew thyself.

Lift up thyself, thou judge of the earth: render a reward to the proud.

LORD, how long shall the wicked, how long shall the wicked triumph?

Psalm 94:1 King James Bible

ONE

THE ONLY SOUND WAS THE CREAKING OF THE SACK AS it swung, listless on its chains. The birds had been going crazy with their bedtime chatter, but as the sun had touched the tips of the Wind River Mountains over in the east they had gone quiet. I had stopped beating the sack and, sweating in the cool evening breeze, I had grabbed a towel and sat on the steps of my new house. The house that had belonged to Ash before he died.

I heard a footfall on the decking behind me and turned to look. Doc Claire Erickson was emerging from the house with two cold beers. She smiled, sat beside me and gave me a lingering kiss on the mouth. It was something I was having to get used to. It wasn't all that hard.

She linked her arm through mine and rested her head on my shoulder. It was a brief moment, but it was a moment of that feeling I had been searching for all my life. I smiled and touched her hair. After a moment of silence she said, "There is something I need to talk to you about."

I smiled down at her. "Is this that 'sit down we need to talk' conversation? We've only been living together for a month."

"No, of course not, I have never been happier, Harry." Then she tilted her head, sighed and shrugged. "Well, yes and no."

"Seriously?"

She straightened up. "Don't worry. It's nothing serious. It's just that, I've been offered a job. It's only for six months. I wouldn't even consider it, only," she turned to examine my face, "it's helping children and families who have suffered the consequences of recent war or civil conflict. There is so much of that these days, and there are so many children suffering."

I nodded and took a pull on my beer. "Where?"

"Burunda. I'd never even heard of it. It's between the Congo and Uganda."

I nodded again and looked down the long path where, not so long ago, I had watched Sheriff Seth Levi approach in his Jeep. I said:

"Is the organization called Better Tomorrows?"

She turned, surprised. "How on Earth did you know? Harry! Have you been reading my mail?"

I laughed. "Of course not. They wrote to me too. That's a very dangerous part of the world, Claire. Especially for attractive young female doctors. The president, George Majok, is known to be extremely corrupt and despotic. The crime rate is through the roof."

She looked away and straightened her back. "Don't patronize me, Harry."

"I am not patronizing you, Claire. It's a statistical fact."

Her cheeks flushed. "Oh, *your* job wasn't dangerous?"

I nodded, still gazing at the gate a quarter of a mile away. "Yup. Did you ask me to quit?"

She sighed. "Yes—"

"Did I quit?"

"Yes. You did. I'm sorry. But Harry, this is important to me. I have wanted to do something like this since college, and I have never had the chance. It is just six months—"

"You don't need my permission, Claire."

"I don't *want* your permission. But as a couple we need to agree on things like this. Otherwise what the hell are we doing together? What I *do* want, and I know it's a lot to ask, Harry, I want your blessing."

My jaw seemed to be cemented shut. I took a deep breath and tried to force something positive out of my mouth. But it wasn't happening. I shook my head, shrugged and spread my hands.

"My blessing? I'm not a priest or a holy man. The best I can do is my support and my backing."

She sighed. "What did they write to you about?"

"They wanted a donation, and they wanted to know if I would consider some kind of position on the board of trustees."

Her jaw dropped and her eyebrows shot up. "But, Harry, that's fantastic! You've always wanted to do something like that. When were you going to tell me?"

"Now, but you got there first."

She shifted her position so she was facing me and grabbed my hand in both of hers. "But, this is wonderful! We could go together! You could teach. You have so many skills you could share!"

"You have no idea how dangerous it is in that part of the world, Claire. I wish you'd—"

"Harry, it's a British protectorate. They have a governor and the British Army is out there, along with Oxfam, and apparently the crime rate is lower than the neighboring countries."

"Lower than South Sudan, Uganda and the Democratic Republic of the Congo is not much of a guarantee. We were going to get married, remember?"

"Of course I remember. And we can have a wonderful wedding when we get back."

"Wonderful, in the November snow. Will you do me a favor, Claire? Will you think about it for twenty-four hours? Islamic jihadists are very active down there. They come over the border from Sudan. For them murder and rape are routine, and if you're an American woman you are beneath contempt. If we go, you need to be fully aware of the risks we are taking."

"OK, I'll think about it. And if I still want to go tomorrow?"

"I'll make the donation and accept their offer on the condition I can accompany you wherever you're going on your six-month posting. But I want a promise from you. You told me you wanted me to give up my work because it was dangerous. What you want to do is at least as dangerous as what I did. So if we do this, that's it."

"I promise."

There was no "if" about it. She had made up her mind and I had known from the moment she mentioned it that she intended to go. And where I probably would not have accepted a post on the board of trustees, as it was I made a very handsome donation and made it clear it was conditional on my accompanying Claire wherever she was sent. They were understanding and accommodating, and within a couple of weeks Claire had her flight booked to Apodo-Djamu International Airport, in the Republic of Burunda.

I had wanted to travel with her, but I had stuff I wanted to attend to first in New York, and the board had wanted an urgent meeting with me before I departed. So I had booked a private long-range air taxi from Teterboro, in New Jersey, and arranged to meet with Luis Gabriel Camacho and Jean Fenlon, two of the senior trustees, at their offices on the sixteenth floor of an office block on 5th Avenue and East 69th, before my departure.

At Jackson Hole airport, as the early sun was turning the horizon blood red, I kissed Claire and saw her off at departures. She clung to me hard and whispered in my ear, "*Don't be long.*"

"I've chartered a Bombardier 800. It has actual beds and is almost supersonic," I told her. "I might even get there before you."

She laughed and started to cry, then thumped me on the chest a couple of times. "At the Imperial Victoria Hotel, on Independence Avenue. We have the Honeymoon Suite. You be there."

"You know it."

"You *will* be there."

"You know I will."

"I'm scared."

"I'll have a martini waiting for you in the bar, and a bottle of champagne in the room."

She gave me another kiss and hurried through security. I saw her turn and wave, and then she was gone. I felt a twist of nausea. The voice in my head told me I should have been firmer and stopped her from going. But I knew that would have been as good as holding a gun to our marriage and pulling the trigger, before we'd even walked up the aisle. At least this way I could be close to her and look out for her if anything happened.

Nothing would happen. I told myself that. Hundreds of people did this kind of thing every year and nothing happened. College kids did it to gain experience when they left university. It was no more dangerous than taking a walk in Soundview Park at dusk. I thought about that and didn't feel much better.

I had an air taxi booked for New Jersey and we probably took off before Claire did. The flight to Teterboro by private charter was slightly over three and a half hours, and we touched down at 11:30 AM. On the way I had looked into all the material I could get my hands on relating to Better Tomorrows. I don't trust charity organizations as a matter of principal. I think once you create an organization, you automatically create something that is more important than the people you're trying to help, and you also create the conditions for corruption.

And that's just the beginning. After that you start creating positions like CEOs, trustees, heads of department, directors and managers, and each post brings with it personal ambition, private interests and the urge for greater power. Each post is another nail in the coffin of your good intentions. But this gang didn't seem any worse than others I'd come across, and in any case, I was not in it for the charity. I was in it to protect Claire.

We touched down in a squeal of tortured tires and airbrakes, then taxied to a halt outside the terminal. The engines died and the door was opened by the stewardess. I gathered my things and climbed down from the plane to make my way through security. I had told Claire I was going to meet the trustees, and that was not a lie. I was. But before I met them, I had arranged to meet with the brigadier, and as I came through security I saw his Bentley parked outside. I crossed the lot and pulled open the front passenger door. He was behind the wheel, smiling at me.

"Harry, it's good to see you again. How's Claire?"

I climbed in beside him and pulled the door closed.

"It's one of the things I wanted to talk to you about. Right about now she's on her way to Apodo-Djamu, in Burunda. And she is about one tenth as scared as I am. So that makes her," I paused and nodded, looking out at the parking lot, "terrified."

It was typical of the brigadier that he made no comment, but simply fired up the big beast and pulled out onto Industrial Avenue. He turned right then toward Sylvan Avenue, the George Washington Bridge and Manhattan. It wasn't till we'd crossed the creek and were cruising up Route 9 toward the turnpike that he finally said, "What made her decide to go to Africa?"

"We're both going."

He glanced at me. "But you decided you wanted to have a chat with me first? What's this about, Harry?"

"I'm not sure. Maybe nothing. Better Tomorrows, a charitable organization that helps kids and families who are the victims of war. They reached out to Claire to do six months in Burunda, and at the same time they asked me for a donation and offered me a place on the board of trustees."

"Did that strike you as odd?"

I shrugged. "Not especially. I've been poking around some of the smaller charities. I've even set up a couple. I guess my name reached them."

He nodded. "So you decided you'd accept the offer so you could be with Claire and look after her."

"That's about the size of it."

He grunted. "Obviously you explained to her it's one of the most dangerous places on the planet right now. All its three borders are disputed, of course, though so far the disputes have been at a diplomatic level. But there is a significant Shiite population within Burunda who are quite active at the moment. It's a British protectorate, of course, and that gives it some stability. But our military presence is really quite small. We have more troops in South Sudan and Kenya than in Burunda.

"There is also a lot of violent crime, murder and rape. I'd say there is also a high potential for civil unrest that could spread across from South Sudan and Tubdhaawi in the north, on the border with Ethiopia." He was quiet for a moment, then asked, "Is that what you wanted, some intel on the situation out there?"

"Yeah, that's helpful. But I guess, when we last talked, we left things in the air. I guess I wanted to let you know that, when we come back from Burunda, I am going to retire. I'll work the ranch, I might even have kids and write my memoirs."

He nodded and smiled. "Good. We'll miss you, of course. I've known some good operatives, but you're among the best. And you know we'll always be here for you, if you should need any help."

"I appreciate it. Same goes."

"I thought lunch at Keens if you have time." I nodded. He went on, "Are you satisfied that Better Tomorrows is legit?"

"From what I have seen so far they seem to be above board. I have a meeting with two senior trustees later this afternoon."

"Good. I'll make some inquiries if you like, let you know what I find." We were moving down Broadway and turned onto West 36th. "You should have a think, Harry, before you swap your sword for a ploughshare, about who is left out there who would want to hurt you." He laughed suddenly as he pulled up a few yards from the restaurant. "Of course Jane would say that you had not left anyone alive who might want to hurt you!" The laughter faded from his face and he gently thumped the steering wheel with his palm. "But give it some thought. It's always a risk with us, when we retire."

He climbed out and I followed.

TWO

Lunch was brief. We drank wine by the glass instead of by the bottle and had just one, small whiskey with coffee. We discussed the future, enemies who might want to get even with me, the political dynamics in central and northeastern Africa, and who I could call on if things got tough. He told me there were a couple of hundred British troops out there, at the Embassy and helping train the Burunda army.

"But the Regiment's not there." He held my eye. "If things go south, I'm afraid you'll be on your own."

By three o'clock I was climbing out of a cab on the corner of 5th Avenue and East 69th. The lobby was all shiny, toffee-colored marble, the elevator doors were beaten bronze and there were ferns and palms in urns big enough to live in.

On the 16th floor I stepped out directly into Better Tomorrows' lobby. I was the only passenger in the elevator and the only person in the lobby, besides the receptionist. I stood a moment looking around. The broad expanse of carpet was burnt sienna, the reception desk was a huge hunk of green marble, there were a couple of coffee tables discretely positioned behind large palms.

The walls were a pale beige but held huge canvasses depicting wild, impressionist jungle scenes in vibrant reds, yellows, blues and greens. The place stank of money.

The pretty girl behind reception was watching me and smiling. I smiled back and approached. She was wearing a sweatshirt with a picture of a cannabis leaf on it. It bore the legend, "Believe Nothing Till It's Officially Denied." She also had her hair in a ponytail and a ring in her nose that made me want to give her my handkerchief.

"Hi," she said, like she meant it.

"I have an appointment with Luis Camacho and Jean Fenlon. My name is—"

"Harry Bauer, they're expecting you, Mr. Bauer. If you'll give me one..." She didn't finish. She pressed a button and put a phone to her ear. "Hey, Jean, Mr. Bauer is here?" She made it sound like a question, then grinned. "OK, I'll tell—" She stopped and laughed harder, then showed me her teeth and told me, "She'll be with you right—oh! Here she is!"

I turned as a section of beige wall swung open and a woman emerged. She had crazy dark hair in what looked like a loose Afro, high cheekbones and startling, deep blue eyes. You couldn't describe her as anything but beautiful, and she had the kind of easy, spontaneous smile that made you want to be around her.

"Mr. Bauer, I'm Jean. It's good of you to come at such short notice, and I know you would much rather be with your wife." She took my hand and shook it with both of hers. "Please, won't you come through? Luis is anxious to meet you. We are really thrilled to have you onboard."

I followed her down a beige and dark wood corridor with concealed lighting, past appropriately ethnic pictures on the walls, and into a room at the end that was large and had panoramic views of 5th Avenue and Central Park. A long, oval table stood in the middle with a dozen chairs ranged around it. There was one guy sitting there. He stood up as I came in and smiled, extending his hand.

He wasn't what I had expected. With a name like Luis Camacho I had expected him to look Latino. But this guy was as tall as me, with blond hair, blue eyes and pale skin. He even had freckles. If you'd told me his name was Shamus McTavish I wouldn't have batted an eyelid.

He had strong hands and a good grip.

"Harry! I suppose we should be on first-name terms, right? Please, sit. Coffee? Tea? We are so pumped to have you with us." I opened my mouth to speak as I sat but he stopped me. "And your donation! Generous doesn't cover it. It will make such a difference to so many children and families."

I nodded. "I'm happy to help. Luis."

Jean spoke up. "There are just a couple of things, Harry. And please don't take this amiss, we have all had to go through this process because of the very delicate nature of our enterprise. Do you mind answering a couple of questions?"

I leaned back in my chair, frowning at her. "No, but I seem to remember you approached me, and you didn't have a problem accepting my donation. If you don't like my answers are you going to give me back the money?"

Jean became serious, but Luis threw back his head and laughed out loud.

"Harry! Harry! Please don't take offence. As Jean says, we have all had to answer these questions. There is no question of not liking the answers, but we do have to know who we have on the board, because we deal in such volatile situations. Our first and greatest concern is the children and their families."

I nodded, turned my attention to Jean and said, "Shoot."

She gave a tight smile. "You were in the British Army for a few years. Can you tell me about that?"

I shrugged. "There isn't much to tell. I was young, I came from a broken family. I don't remember my father. He disappeared when I was just two. My mother was an alcoholic and occasional drug abuser. So as soon as I had the chance I left home, left the country and joined the most bad-ass unit I could find.

That was the British Special Air Service. I was with them for eight years, and they are still like a family to me."

She nodded, then wet her lips with the tip of her tongue as she studied the surface of the table.

"You were not asked to leave, but neither did you receive an honorable discharge. You resigned. What's the story behind that?"

I narrowed my eyes and studied her a little more closely. "You do your homework."

"As I said, this is not personal, but we have to know whom we are dealing with."

"We were in Afghanistan. We had captured a man who was responsible for murdering and torturing the men, women and children of an entire village. The women and the female children were systematically raped before being killed. I, and the other guys in my unit, had to watch as this happened. When we caught this guy, the CIA turned up and wanted to take him away. I knew what that meant. It meant he had intel and skills they wanted and they were going to set him up in a safe house with a pension in exchange for the help he could provide them regarding the Taliban, Al-Qaeda and their relationship with Pakistan. I didn't think that was right."

"What happened?"

"I proposed that rather than let the bastard get away we should execute him there and then. The CIA senior officer complained to my senior officer and I was offered the opportunity of resigning and avoiding embarrassment for myself and the regiment. So that's what I did."

Luis leaned forward, with his elbows on the table. "Harry, in retrospect, do you regret having done what you did?"

"What I regret, Luis, is not having shot the bastard when I had the chance, before the CIA turned up. If that disqualifies me from being on your board of trustees—"

"Please." It was Jean. "Nobody is saying that, Harry. You can relax your defensive position. Please remember, we are all about the children. I think I can speak for Luis when I say that, if we had witnessed what you witnessed we would probably have felt the same."

Luis smiled. "My family is from Mexico, Harry. I lived there till I was five and I have returned often. I have brothers and sisters there. Nobody who has not seen those atrocities firsthand can have any idea what it is like. That is why we are here, that is why we have set up this charity. Every one of us has experienced something similar, and we want to make a difference."

I stared at him long and hard. "You're serious."

Jean said, "We're not here to judge, Harry. We're here for the kids. Is there anything else you feel you ought to share with us?"

I shook my head. "No."

She waited, watching me like she expected me to change my mind. When I didn't she said, "When you got back from the UK you were pretty broke. Do you mind telling us how you made your money?"

"Yes, I do mind. I worked freelance on a few classified projects and made a lot of money, which I invested wisely."

Luis said, "That's good enough for me."

Jean smiled at him and nodded. "Me too." Then she turned to me. "We just had those two question marks. Thank you for clearing them up. Now, we know that you were keen to accompany Dr. Erickson in Burunda, and we are delighted for you to do that. So, what we thought was that perhaps you could liaise with Chris Van Hurt and Adolfo Suarez, who are our administrative managers out there, and take charge of setting things up."

"Setting things up?"

"We will provide you with a file. It contains everything you could possibly need to know, from names and addresses to the overall goals and objectives of the organization in Burunda. Anything that's missing, you call us on the hotline. I suggest you read the outline on the way over and then take a few days to talk to Chris and Adolfo, study the file and then take it from there."

I thought about it and made a cautiously affirmative face.

"This would be during the six months that Claire is out there. After that I take her home and go back to breeding horses."

"That is absolutely understood. We are quite sure that a man like you can make a big difference in six months. After three months, if you still feel the same way, we'll send you somebody to groom."

We chatted for another ten minutes while an assistant went to get a large attaché case which proved to be full of all those documents she had mentioned, and included a couple of phone numbers where I could contact Chris Van Hurt and Adolfo Suarez.

After that it was a taxi back to Teterboro Airport, then a short wait while they finished fueling up the Bombardier Global 8000, one of the few private jets that could cover the seven thousand miles from New Jersey to Burunda nonstop. At a cruising speed of seven hundred miles per hour, it was still going to be a ten-hour flight, so I would have plenty of time to do my homework.

As it was I had a superficial look at the file, memorized a couple of names and numbers and noted the location of the organization's two field operations. They had their head office on Independence Avenue, and then they had Project One in the remote southwest of the country in the jungle just twenty miles from the border with the Democratic Republic of the Congo.

The other, Project Two, was in the northeast, roughly equidistant from the borders with Uganda and South Sudan—about fifteen miles from each. Only here instead of jungle it was more savannah, with small, gnarled trees and dry, red and yellow dust.

I had a couple of martinis while I read through the material. Then I had a sirloin steak and a shower and slept for four hours in the large bed provided in my suite.

By the time I had risen, showered and dressed, and was having coffee and hot buttered croissants, it was one AM in New York and in my body clock, but it was seven AM in Apodo-Djamu, the capital of Burunda.

The city, as I looked down on it through the window,

consisted of a high-rise center clustered with tall towers of steel and glass, glinting dark gray and blue in the early sun, and then a sprawl of shantytowns stretching out like a vast spider's web in all directions. Those parts that were closest to the center were almost suburban, with houses made of brick, wood and thatch, with gardens and even swimming pools; but as they spread further from the city center, corrugated metal replaced roofing tiles, shacks replaced houses and the tropical gardens were replaced by patches of bare land with a few scattered cows and goats, bathed in the dim amber light of early morning.

Beyond that were the lean-tos, the collections of pallets and rags that were the closest some human beings ever got to home, where spirits were born strangled and died stunted and robbed of hope.

We skimmed over these fleeting images and moments later touched the tarmac at Apodo-Djamu International Airport in a scream of tortured tires and the surging roar of airbrakes. Then we slowed and taxied sedately to the VIP terminal.

I was clearly expected because the customs officials, who were all wearing khaki shorts, treated me like visiting royalty and waved me through, and told me my passport was, "quite unnecessary, Mr. Bauer!"

There weren't many other people at the airport, apart from men in khaki shorts all laughing and joking with each other like kids at their first dance. It was large, marble, echoing and empty and as I passed, virtually ignored, through passport control and into arrivals, in the echoing emptiness I saw a café with a single guy sitting at a table with a coffee, reading the paper.

He looked up as I approached him, smiled and stood, extending his hand. When he spoke he had that South African clipped rasp. "Mr. Bauer?" When I told him I was he gripped my hand like he wanted to strangle it and said, "Chris Van Hurt. It's an honor. Flight OK?"

He made *Chris* sound like *Cruss* and *it's* like *ut's*. I figured I'd get used to it.

"Flight was good," I told him, "but I'm keen to get to the hotel. I'm not sure if my fiancée has arrived yet. I'm keen to see her before anything else."

"Yuh, yuh I bet. Your bags are in the car. We can talk while we drive. The Imperial Victoria, right?"

We made our way out of the building and into the fresh morning. The sun had risen and was tinting everything with a bronze glow. There was a Bentley waiting and he gestured me toward it. As I climbed in the back I kept hearing him say, "...talk as we drive..." I watched him climb in beside me and asked him, "Has Claire arrived yet?"

"Yuh," he said again. "Yuh, she got here about six hours ago." He pulled the door closed. I gave a small laugh. "Damn. I was hoping to beat her to it and meet her with a martini."

The car pulled away from the sidewalk and we headed for the highway.

"That's something we need to discuss," he said.

I stared at him and the situation felt suddenly dangerous. "What, my meeting my fiancée with a martini is something we need to discuss?"

"No, your fiancée. We need to discuss Dr. Erickson."

My frown was turning into a scowl. "What do we need to discuss about her? And I suggest any discussing we do about her, we do in front of her."

"Well, that's just it," he said. "We can't, because it seems she's been abducted."

THREE

You read about people going ice-cold, but until you actually experience it it's impossible to know what that's like. In SAS training they deliberately set up exercises where a series of obviously correct decisions leads you into a life-or-death situation in which there is no way out. The object of the exercise is to train your mind to stay focused. Those two or three seconds in which the door is kicked in and a dozen soldiers storm in, the window smashes and a flash-bang rolls across the floor, or you see the flashlights ahead in the forest and hear the dogs howling behind you, those are seconds in which you need to be assessing and calculating instead of pounding the wall and shouting, "Shit! Motherfucker!" and "Goddammit!"

It's a waste of energy and what's worse, it's a waste of time. So that is when you need to go ice-cold. When I heard the words, "Well, that's just it. We can't, because it seems she's been abducted," everything went very cold and very still. My eyes shifted to the mirror, where I saw the driver watching me.

I looked at Van Hurt. He was watching me carefully too, waiting to read my reaction. Maybe half a second had passed, long enough to say, "And." Outside I registered fifteen people scattered around the red, dusty road. No one approaching, mostly women, all engaged, doing something. Six houses in close proximity. The doors and windows open, but no sign of people. Another half second.

I spoke quietly. "You want to explain to me what that means, 'it *seems* she's been abducted'?"

He took a deep breath, puffed out his cheeks and blew. It was the first sign of stress I had seen from him.

"Dr. Erickson was met from the airport five hours ago. There was the usual security at the airport, plus we had this armored Bentley and a Land Rover with a couple of British soldiers in it. We had no reason to expect trouble, but she was a valuable passenger and we wanted to—"

"Get to the point, Van Hurt. What happened."

"Right. So we collected her without incident and took her to the hotel and saw her to her room. It was about half-past two. Hotel security is adequate but we asked her if she wanted additional security on her door. She said she didn't, and asked if a six o'clock start was too early. We said not at all and she asked if somebody could call for her at that time because she wanted to be there to meet you at the airport."

"So who called for her?"

"I did, Harry. She wasn't there. We checked with reception and nobody had seen her go out. We tried her cell but it was either switched off or had no signal. Finally we had them open the door for us."

He paused and took a deep breath. I said, "So?"

"It looked like there had been a struggle. Things had been knocked over—"

"Blood. Was there any blood?"

"No! No, there was no blood. It looks like they went in, there was a brief struggle and they left."

"OK, who's 'they,' how did they know she was here, how did they get in and where did they take her?"

Outside the car the suburban houses were giving way to tall, steel and glass towers. The roads had sidewalks, traffic lights and streetlamps, and suddenly we might have been in just about any prosperous city outside Europe.

"We're going there now, so you can see for yourself. The answers to your questions: How did they get in? The lock wasn't forced, so they probably knocked and she opened the door. That suggests she thought it was us, which in turn suggests it happened either just after we left or just before we arrived this morning. Again, that suggests they were watching our movements. Which leads me to, how did they know she was there? They were probably watching the airport for high-value Western passengers. It may be as simple as that, or they might be receiving information from mid-ranking civil servants.

"So, who are 'they'? We are probably dealing with the AJD, that's the African Jihadist Dawn. Islam is a steadily growing force in Central Africa, and for some time now Iran has been nurturing Shia Islam in Burunda. It's a religion that appeals especially to frustrated young men with few other prospects in life. It gives them a gun, a chance to be powerful, as they see it, and an excuse to kill anyone they don't like.

"Which leaves, where did they take her? They have camps in the jungle in the southwest and in the northeast."

"That's precisely where you have Project One and Project Two."

The car came to a halt outside a tall, glistening tower of dark blue glass. Van Hurt was nodding, with his eyes flicking over my face.

"That is not so surprising, Harry. We have located the projects in the most remote, deprived areas of the country. Obviously that is where the AJD are located too." He opened the door. "Come on, let's go look at the room and talk to Colonel Fisher."

The Honeymoon suite was on the tenth floor, at the end of a long corridor with shiny, slate-gray walls and a cream carpet. The walls were hung with brilliant ethnic paintings, and every corner was occupied by some kind of extravagant vase with dried rushes or palms.

There was no police tape on the door. Instead there was a huge cop in khaki shorts and a black beret, with a face like a slab of unsmiling basalt rock. He opened the door for us and closed it behind us after we'd gone in.

We were in a large, overly ornate room that might have been lifted from a French baroque palace. Everything was in burgundy and gold, except the fireplace which was green marble, and the glass-topped coffee table which looked like it came from IKEA. And then there were the drapes, which probably still had seamstresses trapped in them, trying to claw their way out through all the ruffles.

Standing in the bedroom doorway over on the right, wearing khaki shorts, a khaki shirt with epaulets and a peaked cap, was a tall man with gaunt cheeks and a steel ramrod up his back. He was watching me carefully as I took in the room.

Besides him there were a man and a woman in white plastic crime scene suits and a photographer.

The guy in khaki said, "Don't come any further into the room. Are you Bauer?" He approached me and held out his hand. "Fisher, Colonel, we cooperate with the local police. Your fiancée."

I had the feeling he hadn't so much introduced himself as briefed me. I shook his hand and asked, "Are we any clearer on what's happened here?"

"I'd suggest you have a look around when the crime scene chaps are finished, and of course you are welcome to, but the fact is there is nothing to see."

He beckoned me over to the bedroom door. "Don't touch anything. Keep your hands in your pockets. See the bed? It hasn't been slept in."

"So they were watching the airport, and as soon as Van Hurt left, they moved in and snatched her. They were armed because there was a minimal struggle. But they only threatened to use them because there is no blood."

He eyed me a moment. "That's about the size of it."

I glanced at Van Hurt. "You say they make a habit of watching the airport. My gut tells me they knew she was coming and she was targeted."

The colonel nodded. "I agree. It's a tad too slick. The AJD are anything but slick. They couldn't organize a piss up in a brewery without spilling the beer. But this has been very smoothly planned and executed."

I was frowning at him hard. "So what does that tell you? What are you thinking, Colonel? You think they might have an external operative working with them?"

"It's too soon to jump to conclusions, but it is suggestive, isn't it? An American doctor engaged to a rich donor appointed to the board of trustees, and within an hour of arriving she is snatched in a slick, professional operation. It does suggest assistance from somebody more professional and more experienced."

"Iran—"

He didn't answer. He just winced and turned back toward the door. There he said to the room at large, "Let me know as soon as you've finished. Mr. Bauer needs his suite. And I want the forensic report on my desk before the ink is dry." Then he turned to us and said, "My office."

His office turned out to be a two-minute drive away in his military Range Rover. It was located in what he referred to as the Colonial District. The Colonial District was a Georgian palace painted in a pastel shade of salmon pink framed in white.

"Governor's palace. Privy Council office, military police. Used to be a barracks. Too few of us now. Just an office. We're at the back."

He said this as his chauffeur took us down the white, gravel drive, among gardens that had once been well-tended but were now turning to shabby. As we pulled up at the back of the palace, it was pretty much the same story. Its grandeur was fading. Where its function had once been to project and represent the awesome power and majesty of the greatest empire in history, now its purpose seemed to be to ensure that it conformed to all the regulations on health and safety, with institutional, self-closing fire doors in the ugliest shades available to industry, posters prominently displayed on how to save people from drowning, suffocation and heart attack, as well as ensuring that nobody was offended by the fact that the Brits were, in fact, British, though they were trying very hard not to be.

Fisher led us through this series of ugly fire doors, past the posters and pamphlets until we came to a bright, fire-engine-red door that gave onto a beige passage. The door had a brass plaque that read, "Police Department."

He led us through, down the beige passage and into a large office with three desks and a small conference room. There were a couple of cops at two of the desks. One was male and the other was female. They were both wearing khaki shorts and shirts. From there he pushed into the conference room. He moved to the head and pointed to the chairs.

"Please, sit. Coffee? Tea? Breakfast?" He didn't wait for an answer. He bellowed in a voice that had rallied the best troops in the world for five hundred years, "*Penny! Coffee! Tea! Toast!*"

Then he peered at me a moment. "I know," he said, "can't imagine, bloody rough deal. But look here, I know you, um, Americans believe in expressing, um, feelings." He winced as he said it. "But early days yet, never know, best save that for, um, later. Every moment is crucial right now and no time to, err, waste."

"I agree sir, and if I may, I think we need to work on the assumption that the AJD, backed by Iranians or Iranian-trained men, have abducted her and she is being held hostage."

"Good. I agree, so the question we need to answer first of all is, do we wait for their demands or do we steal a march on them?"

Van Hurt, who had been quiet for a while, spoke suddenly. "If we can steal a march on them then that is what we should do. But we know exactly nothing about them. We assume they are Iranian-backed AJD, and we assume they are going to head either northeast or southwest to their enclaves. But we don't know for

THE DEVIL'S VENGEANCE | 21

sure. And we have to be very aware of the possibility that injudicious action on our part could lead to their harming the hostage."

I cut in. "She is comparatively safe as long as they believe we want her back, and they can get something they want in exchange. Right now that seems to be the case. If we can find out what they want, that will be a help. But right now it is not essential. What is essential is that we establish with some degree of certainty where they are headed. How can we do that?"

The colonel spoke quickly, like he was seizing an opportunity. "There is something that might help. But I will need your agreement. I wouldn't do this without your blessing."

"Say it."

"When I saw the way things were going I sent a couple of my boys down to talk to the reception staff and canvass people along the street. It struck me that if they had come from one of the Islamic enclaves—and if they were planning to take Dr. Erickson back to one of the enclaves—chances are they would be driving four-by-four Land Rovers, Jeeps or Toyotas."

I nodded. "Yes."

"Not one hundred percent certain, but the chances are high that they would have come from the same enclave where they were taking her. That being so, for anything between ten minutes and half an hour there was a good chance we had one or two large four-by-fours parked very close to the hotel spattered with—"

I interrupted him, nodding as we spoke the words together, "—either mud and leaves from the jungle, or red and yellow dust from the savannah!"

"We found three hotel employees who were coming on to their shift who remember seeing two mud-spattered Land Rovers parked twenty yards from the hotel at shortly before three in the morning."

Van Hurt leaned forward. His jaw was set and his eyes were bright. "Then they have taken her to the Djombo or Apamwaza region, southwest."

I shook my head. "That doesn't fit. What causes a team who

carries out such a slick operation to make such an elementary mistake?"

Colonel Fisher gave a bark of a laugh. "That's simple. They didn't want to be caught before they snatched her, but they want us to follow their trail into their territory."

Van Hurt frowned from the colonel to me and back again. "What does that mean?"

I answered. "It means they probably want one person for another."

The colonel grunted. "Perhaps. But I wouldn't jump to any conclusions. At the very least it means they want to leave a trail. And that could mean they aim to set an ambush."

I nodded. "OK, but something else occurs to me. If they have taken the doctor you aimed to send to Camp One, in the southwest, and they have snatched her in the southwest, should we be worrying about that camp right now? I would say we need to steal a march and get everything we have to that camp as soon as is humanly possible. They have a three to four-hour lead on us. We need to get moving, fast."

I heard Van Hurt swear under his breath. The colonel stood and wrenched open the door. "Get me the governor on the phone!"

A small voice said, "Do you still want breakfast?"

He ignored it and turned to the South African. "Van Hurt, I need you to get in touch with your office. We need them to second us as many men as they can spare."

A voice came from the outer office. "Governor, sir!"

He strode to the nearest desk and snatched up the phone.

"Cyril. We have a situation. No, don't talk, just listen. Dr. Claire Erickson—yes, she arrived this morning at two AM—do me a favor and don't interrupt. It looks as though shortly after she booked into her hotel she was abducted by the AJD." He paused and sighed heavily. Then said, "Cyril, shut up, there's a good chap. You'll be fully briefed before lunch. But the urgent issue right now is not briefing the governor, it's trying to get the good doctor back before any harm comes to her. So I need all the armed men you can let me have from the barracks. We are confident we know where they have gone, they have a few hours' lead but if we can wrangle a helicopter and some men from the president we can chase them down, get her back and nip this thing in the bud."

He listened for a moment, then nodded. "Good, but make it snappy, Cyril, every minute counts."

He hung up and turned to me where I was standing in the conference room doorway. Chris Van Hurt was just behind me.

"Right, Harry, I am fairly confident that by mid-morning we'll have somewhere between fifty and a hundred men and the use of a chopper. With just a little luck we will have her back at your hotel—"

"I am coming."

"We really don't need—"

"I was eight years with the SAS, I am trained and I have extensive experience in jungle warfare. You need me and Claire needs me. I am coming. It's not negotiable."

FOUR

Van Hurt came up beside me and said, "I'm coming too, Colonel. You know I have experience in the jungle and I am not new to combat. Besides, you need every man you can get. We don't know what to expect out there, especially if they're leaving a deliberate trail for us to follow."

Colonel Fisher nodded, then scowled at me. "But I don't want any emotional histrionics out there." He frowned, like a man trying to decipher ancient Sumerian. "I know you Americans believe in sharing your feelings and all that..."

"If anyone gets emotional I'll shoot them myself, Colonel. Let's just get Claire back." He nodded and I turned to Van Hurt. "Who are these guys Better Tomorrows are going to supply? You have an assault team of nurses and primary teachers?"

He looked almost embarrassed and glanced at the colonel, who went and yelled at somebody to bring some maps.

"You must know from your own experience," Van Hurt said after a moment, "that operating in central Africa is not exactly easy. A lot of aid workers have either been murdered, abducted, raped or otherwise terrorized over the years, not just in Africa, but all over the Third World. So we operate a different model."

I frowned. "Different how?"

"Well, we learned a lesson from the British Empire, specifically from the East India Tea Company."

"You created your own army?"

He shrugged. "Pretty much. These guys are tough. They are mercenaries, drawn mostly from special forces. They won't let us down. You OK with that?"

I smiled. "I think it's a damned good idea. If we'd done that from the start, a lot of good people would be alive today who are not. But how did you get that approved?"

"The Better Tomorrows Foundation hires the services of the Better Tomorrows Security Corporation at a nominal fee of one dollar a year. The Burunda government picks up the slack in exchange for services rendered."

"Neat."

"We thought so."

We spent the next couple of hours reviewing maps of the area and making arrangements with the Governor's Office, the CEO of Better Tomorrows in Burunda and the Presidential Office who wanted it made clear that they would supply a captain who would be in charge of the operation. The colonel explained patiently that the captain would have operational control and he would have overall control, and by noon we had assembled in the yard at the back of the Governor's Palace. Twenty mercenaries employed by the Better Tomorrows Corp., ten regular soldiers and a sergeant seconded from the governor's men and twenty-one men seconded from the Burunda Army, including two sergeants and one captain who arrived informing everyone that he was in charge, until Colonel Fisher took him aside and called me over to join them at the rear entrance of the palace.

"Harry, this is Captain Joseph Amin, of the Burunda Army, he will have operational command of this operation." He turned to the captain. "Captain Amin, this is Major Harry Bauer, of the British SAS."

I frowned and opened my mouth, but caught the fractional negative movement of the colonel's head and shut it again.

Captain Amin saluted me smartly, and said, "It is a great honor, Major. The SAS are legendary for us."

"Major Bauer will naturally not interfere with your operational control, but he will be my representative on this operation and where matters of overall strategy and management are concerned, he will speak for me."

I gave them both the kind of cool, laid-back salute the SAS reserve for the officers they most respect, Captain Amin started bellowing orders and the assembled men scattered to their vehicles. We had two trucks, two Jeeps mounted with heavy machine guns and one Land Rover for Amin, Van Hurt and me, plus a driver.

A chopper had been dispatched a little earlier to scour the road we were going to follow south and west, as well as the jungle around it. I was aware it was a desperate operation cobbled together on a shoestring and against the clock. And every special operations operative knows that desperate, shoestring operations are an almost infallible recipe for disaster. But I was also aware that this was all we had, and I had to make it work. Because the price for not making it work would be Claire's life. And it was with that sobering, terrifying thought in my mind that we roared out of Apodo-Djamu in convoy, tearing at speed through the scattered suburbs and the shantytowns, toward the Congo rainforest, leaving behind us a billowing cloud of red dust.

The Digbo road was the main artery to the southwest, it led across the savannah and through the rainforest to the border with the Democratic Republic of the Congo. It was one of the few asphalt roads in the country and ran more or less straight. So we were able to make progress and, after twenty minutes, as we approached the sprawling town of Digbo, we could see the dry ochre landscape turn steadily to green as the scattered trees grew into a dense tangle of jungle.

Van Hurt turned to me. "It's strange country, Harry. We have dry savannah and dense rainforest. Sudden storms appear out of nowhere, torrential rain, lightning. It's crazy. There is so much water, so many rivers, some haven't even been charted yet."

The captain pointed ahead. "There is the chopper. Ahead of us."

I saw it, like a small dragonfly buzzing back and forth in a steady grid pattern, scouring the forest below. I knew they would not pick up much down there. The rainforest canopy will mask just about everything. It hides movement, temperature and even buildings from sight and from sensors alike. All we were really doing was advertising our arrival. But at the same time, as the colonel had said to me, it was a resource it would be negligent not to use, just in case. If they grew careless, if they got sloppy, if we happened to spot them, it could save Claire's life.

We bypassed the sprawl of shantytowns that surrounded Digbo, turned east, left the blacktop behind and plunged into the jungle. Now we slowed and the road, the width of a truck, became pitted and rutted from the intermittent, torrential rains and we lurched and bumped along at barely thirty miles an hour. Neither was the road straight. It led us first east, then west, then south in ever increasing sultry, humid heat, struggling with spinning wheels up muddy hills, then sliding down into shallow rivers. And at every stage we were sitting ducks for any half-organized gang who wanted to ambush us.

I told Captain Amin to place a mounted machine gun in the vanguard and another at the rear ready to spray the undergrowth if we were ambushed. But we were not and the road wound on through the ever denser jungle, with the pulsing, growing and fading sound of the helicopter overhead.

After a couple of hours, drenched in sweat, we came to a clearing, maybe two or three hundred yards across. A broad stream ran through the clearing and scattered either side of the water were mud huts with thatched roofs. As we drove through the villagers gathered at the entrance and watched us. I noticed that it was not the joyful, playful gathering you often get in remote, African villages. This was a cautious watching, and there was fear in their eyes.

I told the driver to stop and told Amin to keep his men in the trucks. I turned to Van Hurt. "You speak Bambesa?"

"Yuh, I can talk to them."

"Keep it sweet and friendly."

We swung down from the cab and I made a point of smiling and waving. I got a few smiles and waves in return. We approached a small cluster of half-naked men, women and children, all watching us carefully. Some of the women held babies. A knot of apprehension twisted my gut. They had no idea how easily they could become victims. At the center of the small crowd was a man. He looked ancient and had the teeth to prove it. His hair was white and his face was creased with laughter lines. I addressed him.

"Hello!"

"*Bonjour!*"

That made them all laugh. French was the colonial language in the Republic of the Congo, just across the border. I told Van Hurt, "Ask them if there is another camp near here, besides our one."

They all listened very carefully as he addressed them, then they all started speaking at once, pointing west, in the direction we were going. It was like teacher had asked a question and all the kids knew the answer. When Van Hurt was finally able to talk he told me, "They know our camp. They call it Teacher-Doctor Village. But they said there is another village that isn't a village. It's a camp, and they are only men there, and they are worried about them because they have guns and trucks. They want to know if we can tell the president to do something about them."

I nodded and gave the old man the thumbs up. "Tell him we'll do our best. Tell him if those men come asking questions, to tell them everything they want to know."

He stared at me like I was crazy. "Are you out of your mind?"

"How many young children and babies can you count here,

Van Hurt?" Before he could answer I added, "And how many guns." He sighed. "Now ask yourself the same question about us. If the AJD come here asking questions, and think they have been lied to, they will slaughter every person you see here. You want that on your conscience? I don't want these people lying for us. We can take care of ourselves. Tell them."

He spoke at length and they listened carefully. When he was done I racked my brains and said, "*S'ils viennent et posent des questions, dites-leur qu'ils veulent savoir.* OK?"

They all grinned at me as they listened and the old man nodded and repeated, "OK, OK."

Van Hurt scowled at me. "Thanks for the trust. I don't actually make a habit of putting babies' lives at risk!"

I raised my hand and smiled. "*Merci! Merci!*" And as we made our way back to the trucks I put my hand on Van Hurt's shoulder.

"Don't get sore. Some things you just don't take risks with."

"I hear you." He said it, but he still sounded sore.

The sound of the chopper was growing faint, and as we climbed in the Land Rover Amin told us, "The helicopter is going back to refuel. They haven't seen anything so far."

"They're here," I said. "I can smell them. And they know we're coming."

He gave me a strange look, shouted something to his men that had all the feel of, *keep your eyes peeled*, and we moved on, back into the jungle. We continued along for another mile or so, with the road looking less and less like a road at every moment, until we eventually came to another clearing. This one was roughly "Y" shaped, with the right branch leading west into dense forest, and the left branch, less clearly defined, showing signs of having been recently used. Here Captain Amin told his driver to stop. I was about to tell him to keep going down the left-hand path when he opened the door of the Land Rover and jumped down. As I went after him he was calling out instructions to his men.

"Captain." I took hold of his arm. "What are you doing?"

"Please wait!" he snapped at me. "Go and stand by the Land Rover!"

I scowled. "Do *what?*"

Suddenly he was screaming at me. "*Go! Go to the Land Rover! Go over there now!*"

My belly was on fire. Van Hurt was pulling at my arm, speaking quiet and urgent. "You better do as he says, mate!"

I took a couple of steps back as Van Hurt pulled at me and I watched the soldiers pour from the backs of the trucks and form in two columns. The Burunda government troops and the Better Tomorrows mercenaries on the right, across the right branch of the "Y," and the British governor's men facing them, looking confused. Suddenly I was shouting, "*Captain Amin! What the hell are you doing?*" But even as I was shouting, I was looking around at the two mounted machine guns. Then I was screaming at the British troops, "*Scatter! Take cover! Take cover! Scatter!*"

I tried to run to them, but Van Hurt was pulling at me. I saw a couple of men break ranks and run for the undergrowth, but it was too late. The big machine guns opened up, as did the mercenaries and the government men. The bullets tore into them, cutting them down where they stood. Fountains of blood and gore rose into the air as the leaves danced and quivered and the trunks and branches splintered. It lasted a few seconds, no more. It was a few seconds of hell, fury and noise: the rattle of guns and ammunition and the screaming of dying men. And then it was total silence.

I realized I was lying on the ground on my belly. My eyes were locked on a large, succulent leaf that was dancing gently. Just beneath it there was a bare leg, covered in blood, partly severed from the body of a young man with freckles and pale blue eyes. For a moment I had the absurd thought that at that very moment his mother might be in a kitchen somewhere in suburban England, making a cup of tea. And he was dead, with his leg partly torn off by a machine gun.

It was a second or two, but it was agonizingly slow. My brain struggled to get a grip. Van Hurt had one knee on my back and one hand gripping my collar. He was speaking and his words didn't make any sense. He should be screaming at Amin, but instead he was saying to me, "All right, mate. Take it easy. Take it slow now. Get to your feet. It's OK. Nobody is going to hurt you."

I got to my knees and watched Amin approach, pulling his sidearm from its holster. A voice in my head told me if I was going to die, I was not going to die on my knees. I got to my feet, heard a click behind me and knew Van Hurt had pulled a gun on me too. I turned to face him and snarled, "Why?"

He backed up a step. "Take it easy, Harry. There are over thirty men here all waiting for the word to take you out. Don't do anything stupid. This is one of those live to fight another day moments."

"*Why?*" I shouted it, feeling the rage burning in my gut and in my head. "*You didn't need to kill them! You didn't need to bring them! Why?*"

"That is not the question you need to be asking." I whirled. It was Captain Joseph Amin, sneering at me. "The question you need to be asking yourself right now, *Major* Harry Bauer, is, 'What do I need to do to make sure Claire and I get out of this alive?'"

FIVE

For good measure he pistol-whipped me and knocked me unconscious. By the state of my ribs when I came round he gave me a good kicking while I was down, too. The first thing I noticed as consciousness crept into my brain was a general ache in my whole body, accompanied by difficulty breathing.

I opened my eyes. That brought with it a feeling of sickness oddly mixed with relief. Claire was sitting across the room from me on a straight-backed wooden chair. She was alive and as far as I could see she was unharmed, at least physically. What was going on inside her was another story, told eloquently by her sodden cheeks, her red eyes and the piano wire which was looped around her neck.

We were on a wooden veranda with a rough balustrade made from stripped, sanded tree trunks. Palm leaves laid over the top gave a cool mottled shade. I was on the floor, frowning and wincing, trying to see clearly through the pain in my head. To my right there was a long wooden table. Two men sat behind it on a bench, watching me. One was Van Hurt, the other was Captain Joseph Amin. Van Hurt spoke as I levered myself into a sitting position.

"Are you conscious? Are you taking in what's around you?"

It's always a good idea to make your captors believe you're

feeling worse than you are. Most times it's not a hard thing to do. I groaned and eyed him with undisguised malice.

"Give me a minute. I'm still struggling with how I am going to kill you and in which order."

Van Hurt's face seemed to congeal. The blood seemed to drain from it, taking all the humanity out and leaving only hatred.

"I would be very careful about what you do or say next, Mr. Bauer. I take it you have noticed the piano wire around Dr Erickson's neck." I went cold inside and nodded once. "The other end," he said, "is attached to a cable which is in turn attached to a Jeep at the bottom of the steps. The jeep is idling. It is in first gear but the driver has the clutch depressed. If I raise my right hand, like this..."

He raised his hand an inch off the table. My stomach lurched and I scrambled to my feet. He laughed out loud and dropped his hand. "That's good. That's excellent. I think I have your attention and your full cooperation. Now all you have to do is listen and obey, and in a few minutes you will experience the relief and the pleasure of seeing that wire being removed from Dr Erickson's pretty neck."

A wave of nausea made me lean against one of the posts that held up the thatch overhead. I said, "OK, you've got me. Whatever you say, I'll do it."

"Sit down, Harry."

He pointed to a chair opposite him. I pulled it back from the table, turned it so I could see Caroline, and sat.

Van Hurt went on. "Harry, do I have your full cooperation?" Before I could answer he asked a second question. "What I am asking, as I am sure you have asked more than once in your time, as any special ops guy has had to ask at least once, do I need to prove to you that I am serious?"

"No!" It came out louder than I intended and he smiled. "You can be sure I have absolutely no doubt that you will make good on your threats. Right now, Van Hurt, you own me. Keep her from harm's way and you own me. Start hurting her and you start losing me."

It was a risk. If I had been dealing with Amin he would have whipped her right there and then. But I was banking on Van Hurt being smart and experienced enough to know that I was serious. Sure enough Amin sneered and opened his mouth to speak, but Van Hurt put a hand on his arm and silenced him. He leaned back and called down to where a guy was sitting in an open Jeep.

"Boy! Kill the engine. Come up and remove the wire."

The driver killed the engine, jumped down and climbed the steps to remove the wire from around Claire's neck.

She began to sob with relief. Van Hurt watched her a moment, smiling, then turned to me. "You see how it works. You give me something, I give you something. But you have to understand that this can change in a fraction of a second. There are—" He laughed. "There are *so many* things we can do to Dr. Erickson without having to slice her head off like a hunk of cheese! And rape, beating and disfigurement are just the tip of the iceberg. Or should I call it the hellberg? Because it can go on for months. It can go on for years. Not exactly the premarital joy you were hoping for, hey?"

"I have told you I will do everything and anything you tell me to do, and I mean it. But I need to know something. I need to know that at the end of this you'll let her go."

He nodded like that was no big deal. "Harry, this is better than you think. I have two jobs for you. Do them both, and you can both go back to the States and live out your lives like happy little bunnies, living off the land and making lots of little babies."

Captain Joseph Amin collapsed into a high-pitched whining laugh. "Lots of baby bunnies!"

I knew he was lying, but I needed him to believe that I believed him. I glanced at Claire and gave her a look that said there was hope. The look was for Van Hurt's benefit more than hers.

"What do you want me to do?"

"All in good time, Harry. It's not me. This is not for me. This is for an old friend of yours. He's on his way, and he wants to tell you all about it himself."

I screwed up my brow. My mind was racing. "Friend?"

"He needs to rest frequently, and he cannot go out too long in the sun. He is not a well man. But he is punctual and methodical and relentless. I tell you, I would not like to be on the wrong side of his Monday morning blues. Oh, here he comes, right on time."

I followed his gaze across the dusty clearing. There were a couple of rows of straw huts, a cluster of trucks over on the right and a couple of larger buildings that had been constructed from timber and had doors and windows and decking porches. The whole settlement was surrounded by a simple, wooden palisade, and beyond that was the jungle, dense and dark.

A man in khaki trousers and a khaki shirt was limping across the clearing. He had a broad-brimmed, canvas hat on his head which obscured his face. He leaned on a black cane as he walked and there was something familiar about him, but I could not place it. He came to the bottom of the steps and started to climb them one at a time. His face was still hidden, but when he reached the top he raised his head to look at me.

I have seen some grotesque things in my life, but few as nauseating as this man's face. His right eye had been badly burned and the skin was horribly twisted and disfigured, as was his whole face. The eyelid had sagged down, partly concealing the misted, blind eye behind it. His nose seemed to have been torn from his face, leaving only a stump of bone and the cavities of his nostrils. He had no lips, only gums and a few blackened teeth. He stared at me for a moment, then turned to face Claire. He spoke with difficulty, taking trouble to enunciate.

"You like my face, Dr Erickson?" He pointed to me. "He did this to me. And my right leg. I have no right leg. He took it. And my torso. Shall I show you my torso? Better not. We don't want you vomiting. Not yet."

He hobbled around to face me again. "They offered me reconstructive surgery, Harry. They said in five years I might look almost human. But I didn't want it. I don't need to look good for anyone, do I? All I want is to keep the memories close and alive, of what you did to me that night. How you stormed into my house, murdered everyone, and then burned me. You should have killed me, Harry. For my sake, and for yours. But instead you have brought us to hell. You and me, in hell, together."

"Otropoco—"

"Another little bit. Another little bit of hell."

"Maria said you'd called her. I didn't believe her. You should be dead. Nobody could have survived that explosion."

He limped over to a chair at the end of the table beside Amin, pulled it out and sat. "It seems, Harry, that however hard we or another may try, we do not die until our time has come, until we have done what we have to do in this world. And what *I* have to do is make you suffer beyond human endurance."

He threw back his head and made a grotesque choking noise that was all that was left of his laugh. Because he had no lips, spittle and drool spilled onto his chin and he pulled a handkerchief from his pocket to mop his mouth while he giggled.

"It is not so bad, Harry. I hate you, of course, for what you have done to me. But you are not the sole focus of my mind. I have always been, and always will be, first and foremost a businessman, and you will serve my purpose in my next enterprise. I have two jobs for you. If you do them, then you and your bitch can go back to your mountains and try to live a normal life." He chuckled again. "You won't be able to, of course, because what I am going to make you do, in order to save your bitch, will tear you up so badly inside that your soul will be even uglier than my face."

"What the hell do you want me to do?"

He leaned forward and there was madness and hatred in his one eye. "What you do best, Harry. Kill people. I want you to go and kill people!"

SIX

CLAIRE WAS TAKEN AWAY. I WATCHED A SOLDIER GUIDE her across the dusty clearing to one of the huts. At the door he cut her bonds, opened the door and let her go inside. Then I watched him slide a heavy iron bolt into place and padlock it.

Van Hurt told me, "She has a comfortable bed, she will be fed three times a day. She even has books to keep her mind off things. She is useful to us, Harry. A doctor is always useful in the jungle. Don't worry about it. The only thing you need to worry about is doing what you are told."

Otropoco turned to Amin. He spoke as he pulled a large, silk scarf from his jacket pocket. "Go, mix us some gin and tonics. Bring a tray, ice, lemon, gin. You know what to do."

Amin left and Otropoco wrapped the scarf around his face like a bandit in an old \Western.

"I have to be careful of infections," he said, "and my mouth dries out. Something like this happens to you and your life changes in a million little ways."

"You want me to feel sorry for you, Otropoco? I avoid feeling pity for you by remembering all the children you've killed, and all the young men and women whose lives you've destroyed with your drugs, and all the fathers and mothers you have killed, strung up, hanged and decapitated, leaving their children orphaned. I remember those people and I don't feel compassion for the million little ways your life has changed."

He watched me steadily till I'd finished. Then he said, "You are a brave man, Harry, to play with Claire's life like that."

"I'll try not to do it again. Who do you want me to kill?"

"President Napoleon Baba Serviteur d'Allah."

I frowned. "The president of Tubdhaawi? What the hell do you want to kill him for?"

Van Hurt answered. "Don't question your orders, Harry. Besides, he is a very bad man, so why should you care? You like going around executing bad guys, don't you?"

Captain Joseph Amin emerged from the house with a silver tray loaded with ice, lemon, a bottle of Beefeater and a bottle of tonic. There were three glasses of gin and tonic too. Otropoco said, "Let Mr. Bauer choose first. Put the tray down and go and start preparing the things for Mr. Bauer's journey."

He set down the tray, saluted and left. Otropoco gestured to Van Hurt. "Explain. My mouth becomes sore."

He made a strange, wheezing, moaning sound and sagged in his chair. Van Hurt glanced at him and couldn't hide the disgust on his face. He turned to me and with his glass halfway to his mouth he started to speak.

"You will travel to Tubdhaawi. You will pose as an American businessman seeking to invest in Africa." He paused to take a long pull and smacked his lips. "You will arrange to meet with the president. You will kill him and then you will return here."

"That simple. It's great that you have it all worked out for me like that."

He smiled. "We have arranged more than you think. We have your passport, credit cards, backstory and contacts all lined up. All you need to do is step in and execute the plan."

I studied him a moment and it suddenly made sense. "You're with the South African National Intelligence Agency."

"Mind your own fucking business. And watch your mouth. Too many slipups like that and the lady gets hurt."

I nodded. "Understood."

He leaned across the table and laughed in my face. It was a cruel sound. "And I have to tell you, Bauer, I wouldn't mind hurting her a bit. I bet she wouldn't mind it at all, either. A bitch like that!"

"I said I understood, Van Hurt."

"Yuh," he chuckled. "I heard you."

Otropoco stood. "Organize it. Get it done. I am going to rest. My mouth is in pain."

He left and I watched him limp across the square toward one of the larger grass huts.

Van Hurt shook his head. "Weird fuckin' freak. You did all that to him?"

"Apparently. It wasn't what I'd intended. I just meant to kill him. I blew up his yacht with several pounds of C4 placed under the ship's propane tanks. Looks like he survived. If you can call that survival."

"Living like that, it's not worth it. I'd rather be dead. You were working for somebody?"

I arched an eyebrow at him. "I'm not going to bite, Van Hurt, so you can quit trying. I was working alone, but now I am Otropoco's faithful servant until the day he sets Claire free. And after that, I never want to see him or hear about him again. I am not going to betray him. No way."

He held up both hands. "I'm only saying, he's a braver man than me."

"You want to talk me through the plan?"

"You bet. Let's go inside."

We carried our drinks into a large, shaded room with an open-plan kitchen and a couple of cane armchairs set around a coffee table. I sat while he went to a drawer in an old dresser and pulled out a plastic folder which he dropped in front of me on the table.

"You are Raymond Meier, from New York."

"Raymond?"

"Yuh, maybe your dad was a fan of Raymond Chandler. What the fuck do I know. It could be worse. You could be called Dashiell, right? Your address is there. You know New York so your backstory has depth there at least. You are divorced, you have two kids, yadda yadda. It's all there. Read it, learn it."

"What am I doing there?"

"You represent an American consortium based in Texas that wants to mine gold. Northwest Ethiopia, around Asosa, and northeast Tubdhaawi have huge mineral reserves of gold as well as aquamarine, amethysts, emeralds, garnets, and sapphires. But our interest is mainly the gold, because that is what is going to bring him the biggest profits."

"Why?"

He rattled his glass and took another pull before sighing and putting down the glass.

"Because he has a fifty-one percent share in all the gold reserves in the country. You go in to exploit the gold and you will be his best buddy."

"OK. So how do I get to see him?"

"That's not a problem. I am Rude Van Dreiver."

"Is that only when you drive, or are you always rude?"

"That's funny. I like an asshole with a sense of humor."

"Good, I'll try and make sure you die laughing."

He stared at me in silence for a moment, then went on. "I am your secretary. I have been in touch with the TMC—"

"Tubdhaawi Mining Corporation—"

"Correct, to inquire about acquiring mining concessions. They were keen to help and have agreed to arrange a meeting with the president."

"So, if this is so damned easy, why aren't there mining corporations falling over each other to buy concessions in Tubdhaawi?"

"Well, that's simple, Harry. In the first place the Napoleon

Baba Serviteur d'Allah regime is unstable. The Sharia Brother-hood, which includes all of the country's judiciary, are putting huge pressure on the president to take the country down the path of Islamic fundamentalism. They are already halfway there, but the Brotherhood, who are Shi'ite, are heavily influenced by Iran, who are keen to increase their presence in the area."

"But Napoleon is not keen because he wants to court the West so they'll mine and market his gold."

"Correct again. But he has another problem. He has a long track record of human rights violations. Now, with the promise of enormous wealth from his gold reserves, he wants to distance himself from that. But the Islamic fundamentalists in his govern-ment and in his judiciary make that difficult to do. It's not just the murders and massacres from his youth, which he could hope to kick under the carpet; he also has to contend with twelve-year-old girls being forced into marriages and then accused of adultery."

"The death sentence."

"Buried up to their necks in sand and stoned to death."

"So what happens after he's dead? Why is Otropoco so keen to kill a kindred soul?"

He chuckled and shook his head. "I am telling you, pal. You really need to watch your tongue."

"I will. What's in it for Otropoco?"

He drummed his fingers on the table and after a moment said, "Mexor."

"What?"

"Mexor started out as a money-laundering scheme for Gulf. Their head office was—and is—in Panama. They would under-take small-scale explorations for gold in Mexico. They wouldn't find anything, but they'd claim to find X amount, sell it to a phony company in Miami with its head office in Panama. The Miami company pays Mexor ten, twenty, fifty million bucks, Mexor transfers that money to Belize, and that money shows up clean, and untraceable."

I picked up my gin and tonic. The ice was beginning to melt. I drained half of it and put the glass down, fitting it to the ring it had left on the glass.

"So suddenly Otropoco shows up in Mexico, badly damaged and claiming they owe him because this thing happened to him while he was working for them. And what he wants to do is cause political chaos and anarchy in the tiny, unknown country of Tubdhaawi, murder the president and for Mexor, to which he has been appointed as CEO and major shareholder, to buy up President Napoleon Baba Serviteur d'Allah's share in the Tubdhaawi Mining Corporation."

"You got it."

"He's ambitious, I'll give him that."

"Yuh, he's ambitious and driven and ruthless. He won't stop until he's got what he wants."

I dropped a couple more cubes of ice into my drink and swirled them so they'd cool the drink. I asked the question without looking at him.

"So does the National Intelligence Agency know you're working with Otropoco and Gulf? Or are they in on the operation?"

"That is something you do not need to know, friend. And I am going to warn you for the last time, watch your fuckin' tongue, or the lady gets hurt. Now, if you don't want her to get hurt, stop askin' fuckin' questions, and stop issuing threats. Because next time, I am going to have to assume you have not understood, and I'm going to have to prove I mean business. Do we understand each other?"

I nodded. "Loud and clear."

"We leave tomorrow. You get some rest, freshen up. You'll be provided with an appropriate wardrobe and you'll be given a weapon when the time comes. That's all you need to know for now."

He summoned a barefoot kid who could not have been more

than twelve or thirteen years old. He was barefoot but he had on a khaki shirt with epaulets, and you could already see in his eyes what he wanted to be when he grew up.

"Take Mr. Bauer to his hut."

The kid saluted and marched ahead of me across the square to one of the larger huts. He opened the door for me, showed me where the can was and how the makeshift shower worked. Then he saluted to me and left. He didn't bolt the door. They knew I wasn't going anywhere.

There was a table and a bed against the wall, and a couple of cane chairs. My head hurt, I felt sick and the gin and tonic hadn't helped much. I stared at the open door a while, with the red dust outside glaring back at me. I was wondering about Van Hurt, what his game was. One part of my brain told me he was letting me know he was undercover with the South African National Intelligence Agency. The purchase of gold mines in Africa would be a legitimate concern for them, as would the encroaching of militant Islam. And I was pretty sure that if he had not been there, Amin would have given Claire a hard time. Add to that several times where he had warned me to keep my trap shut, but had failed to follow up his threats with actions, and he was looking like an agent undercover.

But another part of my mind was telling me he was looking a little too much like a friendly agent undercover. Maybe he was trying too hard to communicate to me that he was an ally. But then again, if that was the case, why? For what purpose?

My mind went back to when Otropoco had left us, limping across the dusty square toward his shack. Van Hurt had been quick to insult him, and immediately after that he had asked me two questions: "You did all that to him?" and a moment or two later, "You were working for somebody?"

I nodded. That was the key. Otropoco wanted to know who I had been working for, if anyone. If Van Hurt was one of the good guys, he was going to have to work a lot harder to persuade me. I was pretty convinced he was playing a subtle game to get me to open up about my employer. We'd see how things developed over the next few days in Tubdhaawi. Meantime, if he was protecting Claire—for whatever reason—he had my blessing and I would not be rushing to terminate him.

Not yet.

SEVEN

THEY PROVIDED ME WITH FOOD: BASICALLY SLABS OF meat, cheese and eggs. It was high protein, perhaps with the idea of fixing the damage they thought they'd done to me. I ate and slept, then ate and slept some more, and next morning I showered and dressed like a representative for an American consortium, and at nine AM Joseph Van Hurt showed up with a Land Rover.

"I have your luggage," he told me from the steps while I was finishing my coffee. "Let's go."

We followed the route we had taken to get there, in reverse. We passed the village where we had stopped and they all waved as we sped past. By the time we were approaching Digbo, where the rutted, broken path would be replaced by a relatively usable black-top, I realized were headed back to Apodo-Djamu, the capital.

I knew the answer to the question I was going to ask, but I figured I'd play dumb and confirm my suspicion.

"We're flying from the capital? Aren't you afraid some Better Tomorrows employee might see us and recognize us?"

His smile was enough to confirm my suspicion, but he said it anyway.

"C'mon, Bauer! Surely you've put two and two together by now! We are Better Tomorrows."

"I figured, I just wanted confirmation. It makes sense, easy access to hostages if you need them, easy, uninterrupted access to third-world countries with rich pickings and corrupt governments, and plenty of unregulated, unrestricted land to set up bases for terrorist activities and anything else you may want to do."

"What can I say, when you have access to Gulf's inexhaustible funds, these possibilities open up to you." As he was talking he reached in the glove compartment and pulled out a pad of paper and a pen. He spoke as he wrote. "It's not a bad life for a guy who's not too scrupulous, y'know. It's a shame you and the boss can't make peace. You'd be a real asset."

He handed me the pad. He'd written, *Agree. Truck's bugged.*

I gave it a moment, then shrugged. "It's academic, anyway. He'll never forgive me." I eyed him a moment and smiled. "Do you know what I did to him?"

He glanced at me. We lurched out of the dirt track and onto the asphalt and started to pick up speed. He shook his head. "Not the details."

"I'd already killed his distributor in San Fernando. I broke into his house in San Diego. I killed every member of his gang in the house, about eight men, and I forced his accountant to transfer the bulk of his money to me. We're talking nine digits."

"Holy shit!"

"Yeah, I beat seven bales of shit out of him and then blew him and his schooner out of the ocean. Somehow he survived. I don't think he's about to forgive me."

He narrowed his eyes at me. "You did all that *on your own?*"

"Yeah. He was responsible for the death of a friend of mine, and his teenage daughter. I went a bit crazy and I went after him." I looked out the window, remembering the rampage. "I had killed a lot of people by the time I was through."

"You are one dangerous son of a bitch."

I watched him a while, then nodded and spoke quietly. "Everyone has an Achilles' heel. You've found mine and you have me dancing to your tune. I will do exactly as you say. But if ever Claire gets free, or she dies, you had better have killed me first. Because this time I will make no mistake with Otropoco. There will be nothing left of him to survive, and I will kill every single one of you in the process."

He watched me for a moment in silence. Then he turned his attention to the road and we made our way without talking to the airport.

The flight, with Republican Burunda Airlines, was in an old, refurbished Fokker which took two and a half hours to cover just under six hundred miles, most of which was over Southern Sudan. We went first class, which meant they pulled a curtain across the cabin so we were secluded, we had three inches more legroom and they brought us drinks and coffee.

After half an hour of silence, as I sipped a glass of Scotch, I asked him, "Have they got the plane bugged too?"

His expression was resentful, like I'd hurt his feelings. But after a moment he sighed and looked out the window at the desolate wilderness below.

"I get it," he said eventually. "I can't imagine what you're going through."

He turned to face me and I arched an eyebrow at him. "You can look as snarky as you like. I don't blame you. I have never been in love." He shrugged. "I've thought sometimes I'd like to, but I guess I'm not made that way. For me, I'll be honest mate, for me a woman is something you shag and have a laugh with to get your mind off things." He mouthed silently for a moment and held up his hands. "I mean, I don't mean to rape or anything. I don't hold with that. And I get they are human beings and should be respected. I get all that. But that whole, romantic falling in love thing. Not for me."

"What are you doing, Van Hurt? Are we bonding now, like pals?"

"No." he screwed up his face. "Don't do that, Bauer. Gimme a chance, will you? I'm trying to explain something."

I turned back to my whisky. "Sure, go ahead, explain."

He turned and stared at me for a moment. Then, unexpectedly, "You heard about the Jewish guy and the flood?"

I frowned. "Noah?"

"Nah. There's this Jewish guy in a village, and there's a flood warning."

"Is this a *joke?* You're telling me a *joke?*"

"Just shut up and listen. The Jews are pretty wise sometimes. So the authorities are warning everyone to evacuate the town. But this guy says, 'No, I don't need to leave. I have an arrangement with God.'"

"He has an arrangement with God."

"Yeah. So the water starts to rise, and pretty soon he's waist high in water. And a guy comes up in a rubber dingy and says to him, 'Hey, Saul, get in!' But Saul laughs, see? And he says, 'Don't worry about me. I have an arrangement with God.' So next thing the water is up to his chest, and it's getting deeper, and a neighbor comes up in a rowing boat and says, 'For Christ's sake, Saul. Get in! You're going to drown!' but Saul just shakes his head and says, 'I'll be OK. I have—'"

"An arrangement with God."

"You gonna let me tell it?"

"Sure, go ahead."

"So next thing the water is right up to his chin, and rising fast. And a helicopter flies over, and they drop down a rope ladder. And they are shouting to him through a loudhailer, '*For crying out loud, Saul! Don't be stupid! Grab the ladder! You're gonna drown!*' But Saul, you know, with bubbles coming out of his mouth, he says, 'I'm *burble* OK, I got a *burble* arrange *burble* with Gorblblbl...' and he drowns."

"He drowns."

Right. So he gets to Heaven and he goes looking for God. 'Hey,' he says, 'I thought we had an arrangement!' And God shrugs and says, 'I sent you a warning, a dingy, a rowboat *and* a chopper! What more do you want?'"

I laughed I spite of myself. "Yeah, it's good. So why are you telling me this?"

"Because you are Saul."

"Yeah? Does that make you God?"

"No. So far it makes me the guy who issued the warning and the guy in the dingy."

I signaled the hostess for another Scotch. Then I turned in my seat toward Van Hurt. "OK, let's cut the bullshit. What are you telling me? You're an officer with the South African National Intelligence Agency? What, you're undercover? Stop hinting and come clean. Personally I think Otropoco has instructed you to play mind games with me."

He made a face, shrugged and nodded. "I can see why you'd think that."

"You can?" The hostess brought me my whisky and left. "Boy, you're a real empathetic guy. Maybe we can be friends and everything."

He looked away. "You're such an asshole, Harry."

"Yeah, that's what my mother used to tell me."

From the air there was not a lot to distinguish Al-Islamabad, the capital city of Tubdhaawi, from Apodo-Djamu, the capital of Burunda. They were both less than a hundred years old, and they both consisted of vast, sprawling suburbs that rapidly descended into shantytowns, and both had soaring towers of steel and glass at their hearts. The one, major difference was that Al-Islamabad had no colonial palace at its heart. What it had was Liberty Square with a vast, gleaming white palace designed to reflect the Egyptian roots the country claimed to possess. It had sprawling gardens, a pyramid at the center and the palace itself was a mass of columns, fountains and courtyards. It was like flying over the set for *Death on the Nile*.

When we finally landed, the airport, all steel and glass like the center of the city, was practically empty, with the armed paramilitary police outnumbering the passengers by about two to one. Van Hurt had some kind of invitation from the Presidential

Palace and we were waved through to arrivals where an Audi limousine was waiting to take us to the hotel. We cruised silently, as the sun hit the horizon, first through the sprawling ghettos where bonfires were leaping into life, dispelling the rapidly encroaching night, and then among the towering, glistening needles of glass and steel turned mulberry, crimson violet in the dying sun.

At the hotel Van Hurt checked us in while I crossed the gleaming marble floor toward a cluster of potted palms, wondering if that was where the bar was. When I returned to the desk Van Hurt was organizing a couple of bellboys to take our luggage up, while the concierge caught my eye.

"Mr. Raymond Meier?"

I approached. "Yeah."

"Miss Kuku, from the presidential office, has asked that you await her in your room. She will join you very shortly."

I smiled. "Miss Cuckoo? Like the bird?" I was aware of Van Hurt watching me. Apparently this had caught him off guard. I turned to him, amiably dismissive. "All right, Rudi, I'll call you when I finish with Miss Cuckoo. Arrange dinner, will you? We'll eat at the hotel."

The concierge was waiting with a fixed smile on his face. "Similar sound to the bird," he said, "but different spelling."

"How is it spelt?"

"K-U-K-U, it means grandparent for the Lozi people, a wise person. She wanted to welcome you on behalf of our most luminous president."

I gave him a totally inscrutable smile. "You are very lucky to have a luminous president. Our presidents are not often luminous. You can tell Miss Kuku that I'll be waiting for her in my room." I paused. "Perhaps you had better send me up a bottle of your best, very cold champagne."

He smiled, a little like a kind, tolerant kuku. "Oh, sir, that is already taken care of."

"Of course it is," I said, and slipped him fifty bucks. After which I went upstairs to wait for Miss Kuku. There was something almost mischievous about the name that made me decide she would either be cross-eyed and have her tongue lolling out the side of her mouth, or a hundred pounds of hot, dark chocolate with a soft liqueur center. If the president's office had sent her to welcome me, then the odds were on the liqueur chocolate. But as the elevator carried me up to my suite, the thought of Claire sobbing and terrified, at the mercy of Otropoco, made it impossible to enjoy the moment.

All I could think of was getting her out of that place, and how every passing hour was damaging her—and us—more deeply.

The suite was what you'd expect. There was a sitting room with expensive, modern suede armchairs and a sofa. A dining table, a sideboard and low bookcases were all made of highly polished dark wood, and sliding, plate-glass doors gave onto a large balcony with views of the gleaming towers. Night falls fast near the equator and the sky was now a translucent royal blue, with a vast, orange moon bulging over the horizon.

I left the balcony doors open and inspected the bedroom and the en suite bathroom. Again, it was luxury without taste: marble, brass and huge mirrors in the bathroom, and a four-poster bed big enough for a flower power orgy in the bedroom.

I had just started inspecting and hanging my clothes in the wardrobe when there was a knock at the door. For a moment I felt a wave of exhaustion and helplessness. I had tried to walk away from this, for Claire—and for me, because I was done with it, and now here I was, deeper in than ever, fighting a hopeless battle to save her life. A hopeless battle because I knew, as Otropoco knew, that when this was over he was going to kill her and let me live.

There was another, more insistent tap and I went through to the sitting room and opened the door.

She was definitely the dark chocolate option. Her eyes were not crossed and her tongue was not lolling. Her skin was very dark, her nose was aquiline and her eyes would have had Cleopatra trying to scratch them out. She was tall, slim and generously curvaceous. Her hair, very straight and very black, was tied in a loose bun at the back of her neck and though she looked like she should be in a violet satin evening gown with a slit right up to her hip, she was actually in a sober, dark blue suit with a string of pearls around her neck.

"Mr. Raymond Meier?"

"You must be Miss Kuku?"

"Thank you for not making a joke. I know it means crazy in English. And I am probably well named. You can call me Kazima, or Kaz for short."

"Kaz Kuku?"

"Are you going to invite me in?"

"Please come in, Kaz Kuku, and please call me Dashiell, or Dash for short." She frowned and I shrugged. "It's a nickname. I hate Ray so they call me Dash." I waved my hand in the direction of the sofa and said, "Please, sit. I believe I have some champagne chilling somewhere. Will you have a glass?"

"Yes." She sat extremely gracefully and added, "I am here to prime you for your visit tomorrow morning with the president."

I had found a small kitchenette through a sliding door beyond the dining table. In it there was a fridge and in the fridge there was a bucket of ice with a bottle of reasonable Dom Pérignon in it.

"Prime me," I said, setting the bucket on the table with two glasses lying in the ice. "You mean on palace protocol?"

"No," she said, "on the president's behavior. He is liable to have psychotic breaks if things do not go his way, or if he disapproves of somebody's behavior. If he perceives something as illogical, it can drive him into an hysterical fit, and that in turn can lead to the onset of a psychotic break. And then," she smiled, "anything can happen."

The cork popped, I filled our glasses and handed her hers by the stem.

"How fascinating," I said, "Here's to tomorrow!"

EIGHT

"Napoleon is out of his mind."

"Napoleon? You're on first-name terms with him?"

"In private, yes. In public it is Your Magnificence Shining Light of Africa Most Mighty Herald of the Dawn."

"All of that, every time?"

She sipped her champagne, reclining back on the sofa, letting her eyes rove over me.

"Not every time. It depends on the occasion. Sometimes he is just His Magnificence."

I smiled. "Sometimes that happens to me, too. I am only my magnificence."

She smiled like I wasn't really funny but she had to be polite.

"You should take this seriously. President Napoleon venerates..." She trailed off, watching my face. "That is not too strong a word. He venerates violence. He loves it, he has an almost religious regard for it, and he has a deep respect for those who use violence skillfully."

"You're not talking about Bruce Lee or Manny Pacquiao—"

"No, I am talking about Julius Cesar, the Duke of Wellington, Francisco Franco, Stalin. Men who administered violence with skill and did not fall victim to their own violence."

I pulled the bottle out of the ice and refilled our glasses before crunching it back in again.

"I am not really sure why you're telling me this."

She sipped, then licked her lips with a very pink tongue.

"Because he will test you, and however interested he may be in having an American consortium exploit the country's gold, if he does not respect your manhood, if he does not respect you as what he thinks of as a warrior, he will not deal with you. He will treat you like dirt."

I nodded a few times. "It's not as crazy as it sounds. You get me like that in every walk of life, from the building site to the Oval Office. Oddly enough, where you least find them is in special ops regiments. OK, I'll bear it in mind."

She sat forward and placed her glass on the table. "It's a very fine line, Dash. Don't be insolent or disrespect him. He will have you fed to the crocodiles." I laughed and she shook her head. "That is not figurative. I mean it literally. He has a private safari park where he likes to hunt. He has crocodiles there and if anyone treats him with what he considers a lack of respect, he takes them hunting and feeds them to the crocodiles."

I drained my glass and set it on the table. "Well, it seems we're not in Kansas anymore."

She gave her head a little shake. "This is about as remote as you can get on this planet without going to the poles. And here, Napoleon is the law and, to paraphrase the movie, nobody cares if you scream."

She stood. I stood too. There was a strange look in her eye. She came around the coffee table and stood close to me. "I went to university in London, Mr. Meier—"

"I'm Mr. Meier now? Was it something I said?"

She ignored me, like I hadn't spoken. "My father was a dentist and my mother was a schoolteacher. They struggled and worked hard all their lives to send me to the London School of Economics. I got my degree in law, started my master's and converted to a PhD in legal philosophy, jurisprudence. During that time Napoleon came to power on an Islamic ticket, my parents were arrested, I came home to fight for their release, only to discover that as long as they were in prison, he owned me."

"I'm sorry to hear that, Kuku."

"Now they are dead. I heard from a source, they have been dead for about a year. I found out a couple of months ago."

"Why are you telling me this?"

"Because I hadn't told you that, as well as being sent to prepare you for palace protocol, I was also sent as a gift. I am yours as long as you are here."

Her eyes were defiant. I gave a single nod and felt oddly sick.

"I have a fiancée," I said, "and I am pretty faithful."

"If I do not give myself to you, I will be whipped."

"Well, why don't I sleep on the sofa, and you sleep in the bed, and tomorrow you can tell President Napoleon Baba Serviteur d'Allah what kind of a brutal animal I am. I tell you, I stroll through the jungle and female gorillas just swoon and fall over."

She smiled, then laughed. "Thank you, maybe some other night. Tonight you must dine with your secretary, remember?"

"Yeah, Rudi—"

"Thank you, Dash. You scored lots of brownie points."

"Take it easy, and be careful."

She turned and left and the door closed behind her with an odd finality.

THE NEXT DAY at ten AM a Rolls Royce arrived at the hotel to transport us to the Presidential Palace. Van Hurt and I had talked over dinner the night before. He had been curious about what Kuku had had to say. He hadn't reacted much when I told him, but I got the impression he was just playing his cards close to his chest. I'd asked him, "How do you want me to play it?"

He'd thought about it while he ate and finally shrugged and shook his head. "You've been around the block a few times. Best thing you can do is play it by ear, mate. You know what's required."

Now we cruised in through the big gates flanked by armed guards carrying AK-47s and rolled along the broad red driveway toward the marble steps that led to the vast mastaba entrance to the palace.

Two guards flanked the doorway and two more ran smartly down the steps to open the doors for us. They saluted as we climbed out and escorted us up the steps to where Kuku was waiting to receive us. She smiled warmly at me, took my hand in both of hers and spoke in a voice you could only describe as husky.

"Dash, it's so good to see you again."

I felt rather than saw Van Hurt look at me and frown. "Dash...?"

Kuku pretended he wasn't there. I figured it was the way they did things in Tubdhaawi and following the old adage about being in Rome, I figured I'd pretend he wasn't there too.

She led us into a vast, circular hall with a white marble floor. Flanking the walls were statues of naked men performing various forms of the martial arts, from sidekicks to sword fighting and hurling spears. A broad staircase ascended from the middle of the floor to a deep galleried landing lined with paintings, all of the same man. Some were in the heroic style of the Renaissance, depicting warlike deeds, others were in a more formal portrait style, showing the man at home with his wives and children, or in his study, surrounded by books.

As we climbed the stairs Kuku gestured at the statues and the paintings. "These are representations," she said, "of His Magnificence the Shining Light of Africa, the Most Mighty Herald of the Dawn. He is the supreme master of all he does. He has over twenty children from ten wives, and he is reputed to have killed over one hundred men with his own hands. He is a true hero of the twenty-first century."

"A man's might," said Van Hurt, "is measured by how he disposes of his enemies."

We both ignored him.

At the top of the stairs we turned right and followed a red carpet down a broad corridor to a magnificent set of walnut door that must have been fifteen feet high. They were flanked by guards, legs akimbo, holding bayonets. Kuku turned to me and said softly, "Please wait here, Dash."

She pushed through the doors, barely opening them, and Van Hurt turned to me. "What are you playing at/"

I eyed him coldly. "Excuse me?"

"Why are you cutting me out?"

"Don't even think about being impertinent, Rudi, or I'll have you flogged as an example. Kindly remain silent and don't interrupt us again when we are speaking. And I'll thank you to call me Mr. Meier. Know your place, Rudi."

His jaw sagged and I turned back to the tall double doors. A moment later Kuku slipped back out and said, "Please, come in."

I followed her into a large room with a high ceiling. The walls were of black marble, except that the left wall was made of glass and overlooked a large exotic garden with fountains and palm trees bisected by rambling paths. Before the plate-glass wall there was a pool some twenty or twenty-five feet long and about fifteen feet across. In it were fish and exotic seaweeds growing out of colorful gravel and rocks.

Directly ahead of me was a very large redwood desk. Behind that was a gigantic Tubdhaawi flag and an equally gigantic portrait of the president, dressed in a lion skin and holding a spear. Facing the desk there were two black, leather armchairs either side of an ebony coffee table.

Kuku put her hands together like she was praying and bent a little at the knees.

"His Magnificence the Shining Light of Africa, the Most Mighty Herald of the Dawn, has not chosen to come right now. Will you please sit and make yourselves comfortable? If you would like tea or coffee, or anything else, please tell me and I will bring it for you."

I frowned, and after a moment's thought I scowled at Van Hurt. I asked Kuku, "What do you mean, he hasn't chosen to be here?"

"Please forgive me for not explaining correctly. His Magnificence the Shining Light of Africa, the Most Mighty Herald of the Dawn is a divine being and is driven by his divine impulses. Sometimes he will engage in behaviors that ordinary mortals do not comprehend. His purpose is only known to him. Sometimes it may be to test somebody, their faith or their courage, for example, or their metal. Or it may be some other reason beyond our understanding."

My frown deepened. "So when will we see him?"

"Only he knows that. Maybe now, maybe never."

I turned to face Van Hurt. "What have you done, you asshole? This is your fault, you stupid imbecile!"

The astonishment on his face was genuine and for a moment I almost felt sorry for him, but I didn't let on. "Well? Are you deaf as well as stupid? Have you offended His Magnificence? The Shining Light of Africa? the Most Mighty Herald of the Dawn? Have you offended him with your stupidity and your ignorance? You stupid, sniveling piece of shit!"

The backhander really rocked him, inside and out. He staggered back four steps, then dropped on his ass. I screamed at him, "Get up! How dare you sit in my presence when I am standing! How dare you sit in front of Miss Kuku! *How dare you sit in the office of His Magnificence!*"

Long before I had finished he was scrambling to his feet. When he was standing I gave him another two open-handed blows (they were *not* slaps) that set the office spinning and temporarily dismantled reality for him. But if he thought we were done he was sadly mistaken. I grabbed him by his tie and screamed into his face. "*Speak! Imbecile! Moron! Speak! What have you done to offend His Magnificence?*"

I swung him round savagely and as he stumbled to keep his feet I tripped him and dumped him on his knees in front of Kuku. I yanked his tie around so it fit him like a noose and pulled.

"Apologize to His Magnificence. Beg this angel of mercy to intercede on your behalf and beg for his mercy."

His voice came like the sound of plumbing with air in the pipes. Only his problem was exactly the opposite of that. He had no air in his pipes. He managed, *"Lees fgif ee, ag-iffiheh...,"* at which point he started to turn from purple to blue. My common sense told me I had to start easing up. Remembering how he had kidnapped Claire and suckered me robbed the matter of its urgency. I snarled, "Is that how you speak to His Magnificence's assistant, you filthy slug?"

I looked up at Kuku, who was watching me with curious eyes. I asked her, "What would you have me do to him? Shall I kill him?"

I do believe if she had told me to I would have killed him there and then without hesitation. There was a rage for vengeance inside my head, not just for what he had done to Claire, but what he had done to our life, our hopes and dreams for the future, before we had even got started. I knew, I had been here many, many times. I knew you never came back from something like this.

But Kuku gave her head a small shake. "I will talk to His Magnificence and explain how important this meeting is to you. I am sure he will understand."

As she turned to leave the room I shoved Van Hurt onto the floor with my foot and gave him two sound kicks in the side. I had had a hunch since Kuku had told us the president didn't feel like seeing us that we were being observed. What she had just said pretty much confirmed that. But the two kicks I gave Van Hurt were not just for the benefit of our observers. He had earned them richly. I didn't give a rat's ass whether he worked for Otropoco, the South Africans or Santa Teresa.

He lay in the fetal position close to the desk. I walked away from him in disgust and stared out at the gardens. I thought I heard him whimper and I walked back to stand over him.

"If we lose this deal because of you, Rudi, I swear to God I will take you out to the jungle and beat you to death with my bare hands."

He started to say, "What the hell..." but I put my shoe over his mouth and spoke over him. "Do you have a good dentist, Rudi? Because I swear if you open your mouth to say anything that isn't 'please forgive me,' you are going to need one, because I am going to kick all your damned teeth in and then *I am going to cut out your tongue!*"

I allowed my voice to rise to a shout at the end, hoping that His Magnificence, the Twisted Twat of Tubdhaawi, might be listening and approve. Maybe I wasn't wrong, because thirty seconds later the door opened and Kuku stepped in.

"His Magnificence the Shining Light of Africa, the Most Mighty Herald of the Dawn, has agreed to see you, Raymond. He is intrigued by the intensity of your motivation."

Six guards filed into the room and took up positions from which they could shoot me. Then a man who was not an inch over five foot walked in. He was dressed in gray slacks. I say slacks because they were not trousers and they were not pants, they were what people in polo neck sweaters and blazers used to wear in the '60s, slacks, with flat pockets and a knife-edge crease. He also wore a cream polo neck sweater and a navy-blue blazer with shiny brass buttons. His hair was a mass of tight curls and his eyes, behind heavy horn-rimmed glasses, seemed to bulge when he stared at me.

NINE

STARING AT ME WAS WHAT HE WAS DOING RIGHT THEN, as he stood in the middle of the floor, while six more guards came in and took up position from which they could shoot me if the other guys missed.

I bowed.

"Your Magnificence, Shining Light of Africa, Most Mighty Herald of the Dawn, it is an honor beyond words for me to be in your presence. I can only beg forgiveness for the stupidity of this slug if he has in any way offended you."

For good measure I gave Van Hurt another sound kick.

President Napoleon El Magnifico showed his teeth and giggled. He thrust his left hand in his pocket, gestured with his right and watched his patent leather shoes as he strolled behind his desk. "Your man has done nothing to offend me, Mr. Meier. I was not aware of his existence, and I have no doubt that in five minutes I will have forgotten him. I was simply engaged communing with God on my balcony, and did not wish to speak to anybody." He gestured at one of the leather chairs opposite him. "Please, sit."

I sat. "I am very sorry if I have interrupted your communion with God."

"We had pretty much finished, and I have to say, I was interested to hear that you had such a powerful motivation to meet. One does not often encounter such intense motivation these days, especially among Americans and Europeans. If you will forgive me saying so, Mr. Meier," he leered at me, "you have been bred to be weak, you have had your manhood bred out of you. There are very few real men left in Europe and America."

I chuckled. "I would not dream of forgiving you, Your Magnificence, for stating the truth. In the last hundred and twenty years the male of the species has become a bonobo in the West." He laughed and nodded. I got the idea he was encouraging me to continue. "For the last fifteen thousand years at least, a man's worth was measured by what he owned, what he had managed to acquire, by his physical strength and ability and, above all, by his capacity to inflict violence on others and subjugate them. Women admired this and chose the strongest men for their partners. But today?" I laughed out loud. "Today a man's worth is measured by how like a woman he can become! How sensitive is he? Does he wish he could have a baby? Does he help with the housework?"

He threw back his head and did not so much laugh as scream.

"Stop!" he said. "Stop! You will kill me!" He sat forward, screaming and pointing at me, "That's it! Just like that! You see them on the telly! The man..." He leaned his head on his arms on the desk, weeping with laughter. He lifted his head to say, "The man..." He made motions with his hands while I pretended to be helpless too and made the same motions. He pointed at me nodding. "Hoo...Hoovering...and...mop..."

"Mopping!" I said and almost fell off my chair.

"Men!" he shrieked, "Mopping!"

I wiped my eyes. "Crazy world," I said. "Thank heavens there are still places in the world where sanity prevails."

I heard a whimper from the floor and looked down to see Van Hurt lifting his head to look at me.

"May I get up?"

"What are you doing on the floor, you wretch? Go and wait outside while the men talk!"

Kuku bowed and said, "If you no longer need me, I shall take this man to the waiting room."

I said, "Good," and His Magnificence used his fingertips to indicate she should go. When she had gone, he smiled at me and said, "Mr. Meier, well met. We have much to discuss. You are a man after my own heart and I have taken a liking to you. Let us discuss enormous wealth and the judicious application of terrific violence."

"Two of my favorite subjects."

"Whiskey!"

It was an offer, but I made it into a joke. "Do you know *all* my favorite subjects?"

We laughed uproariously and he pounded the table with the palm of his hand saying, "I like him! I like him! I like him!"

Kuku came in a few seconds later, went to a credenza against the wall and poured two tumblers of whiskey from a decanter. She handed them to us with a bowl of peanuts and left. I had been pretty sure anyway that the conversation was being monitored and probably recorded. Now I was certain of it.

"You want to mine gold in my country."

"We do. In a side note, I personally would be interested in exploring what other minerals could be exploited, but the people I represent are interested primarily in gold."

He nodded. "You are quite right, we have sapphires, emeralds, opals and even diamonds. You have a proposition?"

"For the gold, yes. For the stones, I can draw one up if you are open to an approach."

"Always. So what is your proposal for the oil, Mr. Meier?"

"In broad terms, we take care of bringing in and putting together the infrastructure—we make the mine, or mines, we extract the gold and turn it into ingots and we market it, and we go fifty-fifty of net. To be clear, first all the running costs are paid, then we split the profits down the middle."

"A generous offer, considering how much risk you assume, compared to the zero risk I assume."

"It's not as generous as it sounds. Our fifty percent cut is non-negotiable. I figure why waste time haggling when we could be out picking up babes in a nightclub or hunting in the forest? I know you're not going to settle for less than fifty percent of the profits on your own gold. You're just that kind of man. You're also too smart to believe we would make that kind of investment for less than fifty percent. So let's cut to the chase, right?"

"I will give it some very careful thought, and I will put it in the hands of the palace lawyers. Meanwhile, you will come hunting with me tomorrow morning, in my private hunting reserve. You will enjoy it immensely!"

"That sounds fantastic." I took a pull on my whiskey and savored it. It was superb. I smacked my lips and sighed. "I have one request."

"Tell me what it is."

"Can we use my man Rudi as the prey?" I gave a big laugh and he laughed with me, pounding the arms of his chair. "We could strip him naked," I went on, "and set him off running through the jungle."

There was more screaming and chair pounding. He took off his glasses and wiped his eyes. "Mr. Meier. It has been a real pleasure to meet a man of your caliber. I must go and talk to my lawyers, lunch and after lunch I must impregnate one of my wives. You must go and have your proposal drafted for my lawyers to look at. So I will see you tomorrow, at nine AM. I will send a car for you. If it pleases you to bring your useless man, perhaps we can have some fun with him. I leave it up to you."

We stood and he reached across the desk to shake my hand. He held it a moment longer than was necessary and fixed me with his eye. "You are happy with Kuku? She has not displeased you?"

"No! Far from it. She is delightful. I am hoping to spend some time with her tonight."

He squeezed my hand. "Good, good! She is a fine woman. Let her have it!" He cackled. "Let her have it good!"

Moments later he was gone. I stood in the strangely empty, silent room and the door opened behind me. Kuku stood watching me, with her fine noble nose and her level eyes. We stood a moment watching each other in silence. Then I said, "You'd better take me to Rudi."

There was no expression in her voice when she said, "You don't want to hunt for him?"

"Not today. Will you have dinner with me tonight?"

"Have I a choice?"

"Not really, no."

"Shall I meet you at the hotel?"

"Yes, seven thirty. We'll have a drink before eating. You'd better choose the restaurant."

"All right. Follow me, I'll take you to your assistant."

I told her I didn't need a car to get back to the hotel. I wanted a taxi to take us to a bar, and twenty minutes later we were sitting in a dark recess in a bar someplace with a couple of beers and whiskey chasers. Van Hurt had also asked for a pack of Camel cigarettes. Now he peeled it with shaking hands, poked one in his mouth and lit up. He threw back his head to inhale deeply and exhaled as he spoke in a hushed voice.

"What the *fuck* is the matter with you?"

I sipped my whiskey and licked my lips watching him. "I'm not the one with the problem, Rudi."

He struggled to keep his voice down. "What are you *talking* about? I didn't do *nothing!* And suddenly you're turning on me and—"

"Keep your voice down. You are seriously telling me you didn't do anything? Let me tell you exactly what you did, Rudi. First," I raised my right baby finger and tapped it with my left index, "you failed dismally to get our target's interest. You didn't study the target, you didn't calibrate him and you didn't prime him. Result? We get here, after all our preparations, and he tells us he is not interested in what we have to say. Why? Because he is on his balcony communing with God." I pointed at him across the table. "You made the *elementary* mistake of assuming that he was a grubby little shit like you whose only interest in life is money. That was your first mistake and it almost cost us the mission.

"Now here's where it gets interesting. I hope you are paying attention. Because I rescued the situation by beating seven bales of shit out of you, on camera. If you had done your homework you would have known that there are few things that excite His Magnificence Napoleon the Nut Job as violence. He loves it in all its forms. Now it was a long shot, but I figured we were probably being watched and if I made enough of an exhibition of you, he might just want to meet me and hook up to take a few loves some Saturday evening. And that, Rudi my old pal, was where you really screwed up. Because you allowed me, your prisoner, to seize the advantage."

His face was blank, with a faint wash of worry. "What?"

"When we arrived in this country, less than twenty-four hours ago, I needed you to help me save Claire's life. Now you need me to help save yours."

He took another shaky puff and flicked ash into the dirty ashtray. "I don't know what you're talking about."

"Do you know what that crazy son of a bitch has in store for you tomorrow? My idea. He is going to have you stripped buck naked and released to run for your life in the jungle, and we are going to hunt you. And I have to tell you, pal, I am really looking forward to that game."

"No, no..." He was shaking his head and holding up his hand. "No, listen..."

"After what you have done to Claire, the damage you have done to her that she will *never* recover from—"

"That wasn't me! I've been trying to explain but you won't listen!"

I snarled. "We'll come back to that. Meantime, assuming you don't get eaten by hyenas tomorrow, when we get back to

Burunda, you are going to find out all about how Otropoco deals with incompetence. And pal, right now, you have lost complete control of this operation. And I have your little balls in a vice!"

To show him what I meant by vice, I squeezed my fist into a compact ball, like I was crushing something really fragile.

I grinned and took a slug of whiskey. I savored it and smacked my lips. Then I wagged a finger at him. "You have less than twenty-four hours. In that time, you had better start thinking about ways to make me happy. Because right now my big problem is do I let Nutty Napoleon kill you, or do I let Otropoco do it?"

He took a deep drag. He was trembling badly. He let the smoke out his nose while he stared hard at the table. "Nah," he said, shaking his head. "This is, this is just getting out of hand. You—" He held up both hands and made a gesture like he was slowing me down. "You need to slow down."

I leaned forward and spoke quietly. "The clock is ticking, Rudi. What have you got for me?"

He screwed up his eyes. The bruises were beginning to show big and purple on his cheeks. "Just, just *wait!* Give me a minute."

I leaned back in my chair while he tried hard to think his way out of the hole he'd dug himself into. I watched him turn a sickly shade of gray, overlaid with a moribund purple hue.

"I'd say your desperate, Rudi—"

"Will you stop calling me that?"

"See? That's why you're a mess. You're not a pro. Your not South African National Intelligence. You're a clown. You *never* break cover, Rudi. Never." He swallowed and for a moment I thought he was going to start weeping. I jerked my head at his whiskey. "Drink, and I'll tell you what I am going to do for you."

Pathetic hope shone in his eyes for a moment and he picked up his drink and sipped. I told him, "There will be a price. But at least you get a fighting chance. You understand me?"

He nodded, jerkily. "Yes, anything, whatever."

"You are going to help me set up the hit this afternoon and tonight. Tomorrow I will tell His Magnificence that you've been called back to the head office or something, and if all goes according to plan, we go back to Burunda and you help me take out Otropoco. Because if we don't take him down, he will sure as hell take you down."

"And you!" His eyes went wide. "He'll take you out too!"

I smiled and shook my head. "No pal, you heard what he said. He wants me to suffer. He does not want me dead. We have a deal?"

His jaw was sagging. He rubbed his face with his hands and winced as he touched the bruises. Finally he drained his whiskey and nodded.

"I guess I haven't much choice, have I?"

I gave my head a single shake. "Nope," I told him. "Not a one."

"We can't do it. He'll kill me and," he seemed to reach for me across the table, "he'll kill Claire! You don't want—"

"How stupid do you think I am, Rudi? You think I don't know you plan to kill her anyway?" I let my voice drop to practically a whisper. "Right now, my plan is to kill Napoleon, you and Otropoco, and any other son of a bitch who gets in my way. If I can save Claire in the process, all good. But don't count on that threat stopping me. It won't." I reached across the table and poked him on the chest. "You're lucky. If you make yourself useful, you might just get to go home."

TEN

I didn't want to stay too long in any one place, and I wanted to be as far as possible from places where there might be sophisticated electronics installed. So we stepped out of the bar and found a taxi, and, on the driver's advice, we went to his brother-in-law's restaurant which was on the fringes of the suburban area. It was a middle-class eatery that served traditional Sudanese food, and you could be sure no political conspiracies were ever spawned here, and there were no listening devices under the tables.

I picked a table far enough from the window so we could not be see, but close enough so I had a fair view of the road. The restaurant was on the ground floor of an apartment block eight stories high, but across the road they were mainly one and two-story houses with high metal fences and steel gates. The road was blacktop, but I knew that just a block away the roads were dirt and pretty soon the suburbs deteriorated into shantytowns. Any government official who walked in here would stand out like an inflated condom at a nuns' tea party.

We ordered a couple of cold beers, a tomato and peanut better salad to share, garbanzo fritters and a couple of *ful medames*—

fava beans cooked with chili peppers and lemon juice, and seasoned with garlic, cumin and other spices.

While the waiter went away to get the food I considered Van Hurt across the table. I was playing a high risk game. The risk was that at any time he could contact Otropoco and within minutes Claire could be dead, or worse. But the turn of events at the palace, Kuku's advice and Napoleon's decision not to show, had offered me a unique opportunity, and that was that if Van Hurt chose to shop me to Otropoco, the risk was greater for him than it was for me. In fact, he ran an even greater risk that *I* should shop *him* to Otropoco for screwing up his approach to the president. No, I was pretty sure that even then he was turning over the angles and he realized that his only option, for now at least, was to play my game.

"Here's what I want you to do," I said.

He glanced at me quickly, like I'd shocked him. He went to speak a couple of times, but his throat seemed to be logjammed.

"You know where the president's hunting lodge is?"

He thought about lying, looked around the restaurant, sighed, shook his head and said, "Yeah."

"You almost didn't make it there, Rudi."

"Yeah, OK. I'm too scared to lie. You got me. This is so fuckin' badly out of control, man. You know, we should just, like, go."

"Go?"

"Anywhere, man. Just fuckin' go, anywhere."

"I'd rather stay alive a little longer than that. You must have a stash of weapons here, right?"

"What? Weapons?"

"Keep this up and I am going to have to start bitch slapping you again. You brought me here to do a job, remember. Did you expect me to do it with my bare hands? Or was I going to tell him your sex life and bore him to death."

"Hey! Take it easy, pal."

"You must have a selection of tools stashed somewhere. Get with the program, Rudi."

"Yeah."

"What have we got there?"

"Couple of Glock semis—"

"Seventeen or nineteen?"

"Seventeen, I think. Sniper rifles, scopes, Couple of HK416s—"

"With or without RPG?"

His eyes went wide. "Are you out of your mind?"

The question struck me as funny. "Are you quite sure you're sane?"

He screwed up his face. "*What?*"

"Never mind. I take it that's a no."

He nodded. His face said I wasn't so much crazy as plain stupid. "Uh-huh."

"So have we anything at all in the way of explosives?"

"What the hell are you planning to do?"

"Just answer the damned question, Rudi."

He flopped back in his chair, mouth open, eyes wide and blinking while the waiter served us our lunch. When the waiter had gone he said, "I dunno, I mean, maybe we could get some. What are you planning to do?"

"I'm a soldier, Rudi. Before I undertake an operation, I like to know what my inventory is. Your success in any operation depends on your logistics. So your course of action is going to depend on your hardware and your logistical support. Got it?"

His mouth was still sagging, but he gave his head a single upward nod.

"What is the source of these weapons? Is this a stash you prepared in advance? Or do you have a supplier here?"

"He's a supplier, but it's pretty basic stuff. You know, guns, basically, and ammo."

"Is he Otropoco's guy, or yours?"

"He's Otropoco's guy."

"Good. So how do you get to see him?"

"He's expecting me. I just gotta call."

I picked up my fork. "Call him. We'll go see him after lunch."

While I ate he made the call.

"Hey man! How's your sister? Yeah? Tell her I miss her too. Listen, I'm in town, you wanna hook up? When? What do you mean, when, man? Now is when!" He laughed a lot, like he'd said something really funny. "That's right, dude. When is *always* now. So listen, I'm having some food and I'll come on over when I'm done. I'm dying to see your sister, man. I've got a friend coming along too. Maybe some of your sister's friends might come along." He nodded a few times. "More the merrier, dude."

He hung up. I told him, with my mouth full, "You're about as subtle as an elephant shitting in the bishop's rose garden."

He sighed. "You gonna stop riding me any time soon?"

"I'll check my diary and get back to you. Does one of his sister's friends happen to go boom?"

"He's going to check."

"Eat your lunch. I want to go see him before it gets too late."

"Too late for what?"

"Eat your lunch."

I was thinking. If this was Otropoco's man, I was pretty sure he was going to have a back room somewhere where he had special merchandise. Nothing this basic would suit an operator like Otropoco.

We finished lunch and the owner's brother-in-law came back to drive us to an address Van Hurt gave him. It was in that same, run-down sort of suburban area where the restaurant had been. The houses were big, with tropical gardens and some even had pools. But they were all behind high, defensive walls with steel gates. It was like the big, expensive houses made up a bad neighborhood. I wondered if that constituted irony. The brigadier would have known.

We paid off the taxi driver and watched him drive away. The read was white, beaten earth and a huge, white ghost of fine dust rose up behind him, like it had timed its big scare all wrong, and now trailed away, despondent and un-feared among the banana trees and the palms.

We walked a block east, and then turned left down a track beside a dirty stream, six foot across and probably no more than two or three foot deep. The banks were red and muddy in patches, like people frequented those spots. To our left there was just wasteland, with the roofs of several houses visible over the abundant undergrowth, and on our right, skirting the river and occasionally obscuring it altogether, were dense reeds and sugarcane.

After walking for two or three minutes along the narrow track we came to a large shack. It was made of bits of packing case, corrugated steel and asbestos all nailed onto a wooden structure of posts and crossbeams that was more solid than the outside might lead you to believe.

There was even a veranda thatched with what looked like banana leaves, and beneath it a ragtag collection of chairs and a homemade bench. Van Hurt hammered on the wooden door, and after a moment it opened and I saw that the inside had been lined with quarter-inch steel.

The man who stood there must have been six foot six. He had long legs and long arms, but his shoulders were narrow and his head, perched on a very long neck, seemed to have been borrowed from a much smaller man. His Bermuda shorts were the color of rust and his string-sleeved vest had once been green but was now just sad.

Van Hurt said, "Bangbang, man!"

He grinned at Van Hurt with extremely white teeth and then went into a complicated handshake that involved a lot of schoolboy grinning until our host squealed and slapped Van Hurt on the shoulder.

"Good to see you, man! Good to *see* you! Where you been?"

He propelled him through the door and turned his huge grin on me. "This your friend?" He gripped my hand and we shook. "Any friend of My Man is a friend of me, OK. Come on in. Come in."

I stepped inside. He pulled the door closed and bolted it, and for a moment my belly lurched and I thought I might have a problem. But I knew, and Van Hurt knew, killing me was not enough. Otropoco wanted me alive, and he wanted me to execute this job. There was nothing he could do but accept the situation as it was.

We followed Bangbang across a covered yard strewn with every imaginable kind of trash, from rusty gas tanks to broken chairs and giant flowerpots. He led us through another door and into a large room with a bed, a refrigerator, a table and a TV. Here and there, there were a few bentwood chairs. The floor was dirt and the roof was part corrugated iron and part tarpaulin.

"I got the biggest house in the neighborhood," he told me. "You want a beer? I got nice cold beer."

"Yeah. Beer would be nice. Listen, Bangbang. You know who I am working for?"

He had the fridge open and he turned to stare at Van Hurt. Van Hurt nodded and Bangbang gave me the once-over. It wasn't a friendly look. It said he didn't like my manners.

"I know."

"So you know that sometimes, if you are going to do a job, what you need is a rock, or a stick." He handed me my beer and handed another to Van Hurt. His expression was resentful. Van Hurt shrugged an apology. I said, "I'm over here, Bangbang. Look at me. You can make a lot of money out of this. Pay attention."

He sat in his chair and watched me.

"Sometimes something basic like a rock is enough, but sometimes you need something bigger, better or more complex." He didn't answer. He just stared. I went on. "Now I know that my employer would not have chosen you if all you had was sticks and stones."

His face was tight. He was mad. "I have no guarantee from

your employer. He is not a trusted customer. I deal with him once, because My Man is old friend from before. But your employer is not a trusted client for me." He pointed a long, slender finger at me. "And if you try to hurt me, pretty soon you going to have the whole neighborhood here, not with rocks, with machetes!"

I nodded. "Relax, I don't mean you any harm. But I can't do business with you if all you can offer me is a Glock 17 and an HK 416. I need more and I can pay."

"What do you want?"

"Sig Sauer P226."

He smiled. "Yeah, everybody wants that baby. OK. If you can pay, it's OK."

"I want the extended magazine. I'll take two HK 416s, and here is where it starts to get exotic. I need a roll of detonation cord, I need sixteen pounds of C4 with remote detonators and tripwire. I need a reel of tough string and I need a Fairbairn and Sykes commando knife, but you probably haven't got one."

He was silent for a long time, looking up at his patchwork ceiling.

"What you gonna do," he asked the tarpaulin, "start a revolution?"

"Come on, Bangbang. You know as well as I do you do not ask that question. I have a job to do, and you have to help me. You provide me with the hardware, I will pay you, you don't even need to put my employer on your trusted list, and I assure you you will never see me again."

Something in my tone of voice must have meant something to him, because his eyes dropped from the ceiling to study me.

"Fairbairn and Sykes I got one, but it's mine. I don't give it to nobody. I can give you a good bowie knife. The rest of it, how soon you need it?"

"Before tonight."

"Is gonna cost you five thousand US dollars. Cash on delivery."

"Not a problem. Give me a time and a place for delivery."

He thought about it a minute, and tipped his bottle to his lips for the first time. I glanced at Van Hurt and noticed his bottle was empty. My own beer was untouched.

"You want a reliable Toyota truck?"

The question surprised me, but his tone told me I really did want a reliable Toyota truck. "OK."

"Extra five hundred dollars. The engine has been modified. It will go uphill through a river, man. Is a tank. And you have three different license plates. They magnetic. So you can change them when you like. I been using it for a couple years. But I think maybe you gonna need it."

"OK, sounds good."

"I meet you eight o'clock tonight in the parking lot at the Al-Madinat shopping center on Constitution Road, just south of the city. You know?"

Van Hurt said, "Yeah, I know."

"There we make the exchange."

I stood and Van Hurt and Bangbang got to their feet. He and Van Hurt embraced to show no hard feelings, but I didn't shake his hand. I said:

"Bangbang, I am sure you're a good guy, and I know you are too smart to pull any kind of stunt, but I have to cover every angle. You know that an operation that uses this kind of hardware is not a drive-by shooting of some guy who got on the boss's nerves."

"I understand."

"I wonder if you do. You try to screw me when I'm buying a P226 and you have a serious problem. You try to screw me on this operation, and there is nowhere you can go, nothing you can do. Are you sure you understand that?"

"I understand. There is no need for you to threaten me."

I held his eye. "I'm not threatening you, Bangbang."

Our departure was more somber than our arrival. He let us out onto the track by the stream and we started walking back toward the suburban area. I could hear chickens nearby, a couple of women talking, the shouts of children playing, and the lapping of the filthy water. Life went on. But what so few people realize when they use that cliché, is that life goes on, implacably, toward death.

ELEVEN

At seven thirty that evening Kuku arrived at the hotel. I was waiting for her in the lobby and as she stepped through the door I moved to meet her. She gave me a kiss on the cheek that would have made an Eskimo shudder, and said, "I told the taxi to wait."

"Good, let's go. Have you chosen a restaurant?"

She might have nodded, if she did it was barely perceptible, and I followed her across the sidewalk to the cab.

We drove in silence through the bright, glimmering lights of the city center, and after no more than two or three minutes we pulled up beside a red awning at the corner of African Liberty Avenue and Queen Victoria Street. I climbed out, thinking to myself that irony is never better than when it is unintentional, and went around to open the door for Kuku.

The cab drove away into the amber night and Kuku took my arm. The gold lettering on the red awning said, *The Colonial.*

A guy in a white dinner jacket opened the door for us and bowed as we entered. It was hard to tell, but I was pretty sure he was bowing to Kuku. The place was carpeted in deep burgundy, there was a lot of dark wood and crisp white linen, shiny brass and art deco lamps. He gestured across the floor with a white-gloved hand and said, "We have the table in the alcove, madam," like he just knew she was going to love the fact that they had the table in the alcove. He led the way.

The alcove turned out to be an oak-paneled box in the corner with two art-deco brass lamps on the wall and sweet-smelling flowers cascading from cute, porcelain troughs above our heads. The waiter helped her to sit, and as I sat I told him, "We'll have a couple of dry martinis while we choose."

He bowed again and went away.

The leather-bound menus were already on the table. I opened mine, but she laid both hands side by side on top of hers and studied her fingers. I looked at them and decided they were nice fingers.

"Would you like to explain to me, Mr. Meier, what that disgusting exhibition was about this morning?"

I had no idea how to answer. So I leaned back in my chair and studied her face. Her eyes were bright. She had tears in them, but she had her emotions under control. Before I could think of an answer, she went on.

"We are engaged in a deep struggle to drag this country out of the dark ages without spilling over into a civil war. We are struggling to cultivate respect for human beings, humanity at the administrative level of government, decency, responsibility and accountability." She made several attempts to start a new sentence, but ended up shaking her head and letting out a little gasp that went with a little frown.

"When you showed up, I thought," she paused, unhappy with the word, "I *believed* that you brought hope. I believed that you were bringing us an opportunity. And then you..." She shook her head and gestured with her hand toward the vision she had of what I had done. "The way you treated that poor man!"

I smiled. The waiter arrived with our drinks, set them on the table and withdrew. When he'd gone I asked her, "Is this some game you're playing? Has His Almightiness instructed you to test me or something?" She narrowed her eyes and I went on.

"Because it seems to me it was you who was at pains to tell me how much the president admired and respected violence."

"Well, if that's the case I wish I never had."

I grunted. "Personally I'm glad you did. Because of that poor man's incompetence we came very close to losing the opportunity to talk to the president. It was on the strength of your advice that I behaved as I did, and now we will be able to go ahead with the mining concession."

She looked away. "My god, to think that you abused that man in that way because of what I said. It's horrible."

I picked up my drink and studied the olive for a moment. I sipped and as I set the glass down again I told her, "Things are not always what they seem, Kuku. Right now, for example, you are seeing things exactly opposite to what they really are."

She hadn't touched her drink and still had both hands on her menu.

"I think you had better explain that, Mr. Meier."

"You see me as a violent bully, who enjoys abusing people weaker than myself. In fact I hate violence, and I really—honestly —wish that it were possible to resolve problems without having to resort to violence. Sadly, all too often it's not possible."

"My heart breaks for you." She made no effort to hide the sarcasm.

"On the other hand you see Rudi as a poor, abused victim. In fact, Rudi is a very violent man who abuses women and children, and that was one of the reasons why I found it so easy to do what I did to him."

She closed her eyes and shook her head. "I find this thing utterly disgusting. I don't know how you can..."

She trailed off. I chuckled to myself and opened my menu. "What thing is that, exactly, Kuku?"

"This deal you are doing for gold with Napoleon, playing to his taste for violence and exploitation, abusing human beings in order to achieve your ends. It is inhuman. It's disgusting."

"Do I need to remind you that you're his personal assistant?"

Her face went hard. "Of course not, but I already explained to you—"

"What you didn't explain," I cut her short, "was how you came to be the only person in the world who had an impossible choice to make. I missed that bit. I also missed the part where you explained to me how you were the only person in the world who was ever blackmailed or subjected to unendurable threats."

She stared at me a long time while I read the menu. When I finally closed it, her expression had changed.

"Is that what has happened to you?"

I made a face like I was surprised. "You don't know?"

"Of course not. How could I possibly—"

"So you don't know." I gave it a moment. "You don't know. That's my point. And my advice is don't make judgments when you haven't got all the information. This situation is much more complex than you know, and if you'll allow me to advise you, keep an open mind and trust your first impressions."

I watched her eyes flit over my face. She didn't answer me. She opened her menu, glanced at it and closed it after just a moment, like she couldn't think about food. We sat in silence till the waiter came. She ordered smoked Norwegian salmon with sautéed asparagus tips, and I ordered *pâté de foie gras* with hedgerow sauce, followed by roast beef. She had lamb cutlets with creamy mashed potatoes and garden peas. It was like being back at the mess in Herefordshire.

As he collected the menus I told him, "And we'll have a Chateau Margaux, Pavillon Blanc, 2014 with the first course. You can put that on ice now. With the beef and the lamb we'll have a Tokara Telos, Stellenbosch. A 2015 if you have one. And you'd better open that now and let it breathe."

When he'd gone she smoothed out the tablecloth with the palms of her hands. "You have this veneer of civilization—"

"I got all my civilized traits from a brigadier in the British army. All the brutality I learned from the streets of the Bronx."

"Who are you?"

"Who am I?" I shrugged. "I'm you. A person who's lost their North Star and is trying to survive a few days in hell, without selling too much of their soul."

"Is that what we are doing?" She rearranged the salt and the pepper and that seemed to convince her. "Maybe you're right." She gave me a smile that was not so cold, but more dispirited. "I'm sorry. It was not my place to judge you and attack you."

"Was it your place to question me?" For a moment she looked confused. "I'm not much of a political animal, Kuku. I find it hard enough to keep my own life on track, without trying to tell everybody else what they should be doing, but it seems to me that if you care about your country, and you care about its direction into the future, you have not just the right, but the obligation to question a man like me, who shows up wanting to exploit the country's gold reserves."

"This is a very dangerous conversation."

"For you or for me?"

"If it was overheard and misinterpreted, it could cost us both our lives."

I nodded a few times, holding her eyes steady. "Let me make something clear," I said. "My admiration for President Napoleon is deep and real, and is based on a simple fact. Very few people understand that the force that makes this world work, the force that backs the law and the world economy, is one and only one— violence. President Napoleon is one of the very few men I know who understands that."

She looked down at the tablecloth. I reached across and touched her hand. She glanced up at me. "And I admire you," I added, "because you are a rare, highly intelligent woman who supports a great man through thick and through thin. I know, and my consortium knows, that you and I are going to work as a great team to make Tubdhaawi a real paradise, and President Napoleon one of the richest men on the planet."

We stared at each other for a long moment and she smiled. It was an oddly shy, childlike smile. "I'm not wearing a wire," she said. "Actually, I am not wearing anything under this dress. You can check if you like."

"There is nothing I would like better," I told her with warmth, "but as I told you. I am engaged."

She nodded. "But play the game. I will have to sleep in your bed tonight. The president has taken a liking to you, and if he thinks I have not pleased you—"

"Sure, you are welcome in my bed." I frowned. "Are you coming on the hunt tomorrow?"

"No, women do not go on hunts."

"You're not missing much," I said. "A few fireworks and the noisy, ugly killing of some dumb animal."

I thought that summed it up quite nicely, and as I leaned back in my chair the salmon and the pâté arrived, along with the ice bucket holding the wine.

TWELVE

THE SUNRISE WAS A RIOT OF FIRE AND BLOOD ON THE eastern horizon. We were in a field of dry grass and low, twisted trees. There were four Land Rovers, a Range Rover and one open, seven-ton military truck carrying just about everything you might need to keep a dangerously psychotic megalomaniac happy, including an entire armory of guns and rifles, enough ammunition for a small war and an entire kitchen complete with propane canisters the size of ICBMs.

And there were people. The four Land Rovers had brought fifteen soldiers from the president's personal guard. They were to form a cordon around us and make sure nobody got close enough to the president to kill him, which I thought was kind of ironic. Apparently this job was all about irony.

As well as the soldiers there were six cooks, two gunsmiths, a driver and a driver's assistant. They were all now busily setting up camp, which involved erecting a large tent and a marquee. The kitchen and dining room were to be in the marquee, and the tent was so that the president could sit down in the shade when he wanted to.

The Presidential Guard would also act as beaters. Because about a hundred yards from where all this activity was taking place there was a dark, dense wall of trees, which towered some fifteen to twenty feet into the air, and inside there were the animals we had come here to kill.

The Range Rover had come for me unexpectedly at six in the morning. Fortunately I had been up and showered and was dressing. When I had got down to the waiting Range Rover I had found the president waiting for me. My, "Good morning," had received a large smile and, "What about Kuku?"

"She is snuggled up in bed," I'd told him. "I didn't think hunts and women mixed."

"Quite right, and what about your incompetent assistant. Shall we hunt him today?"

"There is nothing I would like better, but he has been summonsed back to the head office."

"Maybe some other time then."

We had both laughed savagely and taken off through the pre-dawn twilight toward the president's private hunting park.

Now we stood drinking coffee and watching the African red seep across the horizon, while in among the darkness of the trees hysterical birds raised hell. I stood beside His Magnificence, President Napoleon Baba Serviteur d'Allah, the Shining Light of Africa and Most Mighty Herald of the Dawn. He showed me his big grin from behind his huge glasses.

"You like Kuku, eh?"

"She's fabulous."

"You want her?"

I laughed. "You mean to keep?"

"Sure. You can have her. I used to like her but I am done with her now."

I thought of various things to say, including inquiring about her family and parents, but settled on, "Your generosity is overwhelming. I've never been given a person before."

"I have," he said, pointing toward the tree line. "Happens all the time. So, we have sent in the beaters. They will start scaring the animals, shouting and whacking with sticks, walking back toward us. It's very exciting, Raymond—" He gave me what you could only call a cheeky smile and added, "I know Kuku calls you Dash. Can I call you Dash?"

"It would be an honor."

"I thought you might like that. So, *Dash*," we both laughed at that, "it is very exciting because we have some very dangerous animals in there, and sometimes the beaters get mauled and killed."

I winced and he nodded. "Right? I mean these are not just any old people! They are my personal guard and I am risking them in the hunt. I think that says something about my character, right, Dash?"

I nodded. "It says you are one crazy, brave son of a gun!"

"I think so. And now, what we do, is we advance steadily toward the forest. If an animal comes charging out, a pig for example, or monkeys, sometimes even an elephant, we shoot it. If I say, 'Mine!', then you have to let me shoot it. Otherwise I might say, 'It's yours!' Or if some other friend was with us, like George Bush or John Podesta, or Barack Obama, I might say, 'Yours, Barack!' and so they would shoot it."

I arched an eyebrow. "You get a lot of US presidents?"

"Before. But now I am friends with Boris and the Iranians, the Americans don't feel they can come anymore. It would be bad for their public image, you know." He shrugged. "It's the price they pay for becoming weak."

"You got that right."

Noises, shouts and shrieks, began to reach us from the forest. Napoleon the Magnificent jerked his head toward the trees and said, "Let's begin our approach."

We started our walk. I was about twenty feet to his right and slightly behind him, and on either flank, about thirty or forty feet away, we had three armed men whose job it was to keep Napoleon safe. Their eyes were not on the forest as much as they were on the outlying land to our sides and behind us.

We were two hundred and fifty yards from the trees when we

heard a shriek and a squeal and a large boar, probably eight hundred pounds of pig, thundered out of the undergrowth, plowing through the tall grass toward the trucks and the marquee. I heard Napoleon shout, "Mine!", stopped walking and looked at him.

He had his rifle to his shoulder, his pose was perfect and he was relaxed. He tracked the pig for a count of three and fired. The pig gave a little jump, it fell on its back and its feet twitched. Napoleon shouted, "Move on!" and we started walking again while behind us the kitchen staff dispatched a Land Rover to pick up the carcass for butchering.

The birds were going crazy, bursting from the trees in clouds and shrieking to the heavens, but at a hundred yards a dozen Gambela bushbuck came bounding out of the undergrowth. I heard Napoleon shriek with laughter on my left and suddenly he was screaming, "*Yours, Dash! Yours! Yours!*"

An irrational sickness gripped my belly, watching these beautiful, graceful animals springing across the open savannah. I felt a rage that was hard to conceal at the thought that these beautiful creatures had to die simply because this insane dwarf wanted to kill them. I thought of Claire and knew I had no choice. I raised the rifle to my shoulder, tracked the lead buck and pulled the trigger. The shot went high and Napoleon screamed with laughter. A moment later a shot rang out and the beautiful animal stumbled and fell. Another shot took down the one behind it.

I turned to look at him and laughed. I spread my hands. "I don't know what happened. Usually I'm a good shot."

He was wagging his finger at me and laughing. "It's that Kuku. Women are the bane of good men."

"Can't argue with that."

"Three to me, zero to you!" he called back. "You had better focus."

Soon we had reached the shadows cast by the trees in the morning sun. We were forty or fifty paces from the tree line and I heard Napoleon say, "I hear gorillas. That would be a fine prize for you, my friend. If we see a gorilla, it's yours."

I gripped my rifle with my left hand and gave him the thumbs up with my right. Beyond him I could see the three bodyguards scanning the trees and the savannah. I glanced to the right and saw the other three doing the same. The beaters were ahead of us, in the shadows of the forest and between us and them there was, supposedly, a small stampede of animals headed our way.

I slipped my hand in my pocket, felt my cell and clicked the button on the right-hand side. That was when all hell broke loose. The jungle erupted in a rapid series of explosions, followed by machine-gun fire that spat across the savannah and took out two of the bodyguards on my right. Their screaming and crying was drowned out by another series of explosions that sent clouds of birds shrieking into the morning sky. Under the canopy you could hear men shouting to each other in terror.

Less than a second had gone by and I was racing across the uneven ground toward Napoleon. As I ran I was bellowing at the four remaining bodyguards, pointing frantically at the two fallen men.

"*Gunmen at two o'clock! Gunmen at two o'clock! Two men down! Cover that position!*"

The latter I shouted as I hurled myself at Napoleon. I slung my left hand around his neck, dragged him to the ground and covered him with my body. "*Don't move!*" I hissed at him. "*I've got you covered!*"

By now the nine guys who'd been beating in the forest came pouring out from among the trees. They looked more like they were fleeing than rushing to the rescue, but I bellowed at them, "*In the trees! Two o'clock. Cover me!*"

While they sprayed the area I grabbed Napoleon and rushed back toward the Range Rover. As I ran I screamed at the kitchen staff, "*Get out of here. Grab the truck and go! Go! Go!*"

They didn't need much telling. As I wrenched open the back door of the Range Rover the truck was kicking up dirt, hurtling for the road two hundred yards away, with guys clinging to every available bit of the vehicle. I hurled Napoleon onto the back seat and snarled, "*Don't move! Stay put!*"

Then I turned and yelled to the men who were still spraying the jungle. There had been no answering fire and no explosions for about thirty seconds.

"*Move in! Move in and kill the bastards!*" There was a moment's hesitation, so I yelled, "*Charge! In the name of Napoleon the Magnificent! Charge!*"

People are sadly predictable at times. They knew the president was there watching, so they charged, racing into the dense undergrowth, firing as they went. I knew what they would find. They'd find a beaten path, undergrowth ripped up by automatic fire, an all too simple trail to follow back to where they now assumed the gunmen lay, dead or dying. Instead they would find the two Heckler and Koch assault rifles and the abandoned rucksack. The huge explosion came bang on time.

I turned to face His Magnificence, President Napoleon Baba Serviteur d'Allah, Shining Light of Africa and Most Mighty Herald of the Dawn. He was staring at me fixedly. He knew what had just happened, but he didn't want to believe it. So I made it clear for him. I grabbed him by his collar and pulled him out of the Range Rover. His heavy glasses slipped off his nose and fell in the deep grass. He was almost pitiful, but I forced myself to remember all the murders and rapes he was guilty of, and all the torture that had been performed in his name.

"Take this thought into the next world with you, Napoleon. People who live like you, people who do the kind of things you do, people who believe it's OK to make other people suffer—bad things end up happening to people like you."

His face twisted, contorted into hatred and he lunged at my face with hands like claws. But the broad, razor-sharp blade of the bowie knife plunged deep into his throat as he moved forward. When he reached the hilt I slashed hard right, severing veins and artery, and his evil, nasty little life drained away in a couple of seconds.

I slammed the rear door and climbed behind the wheel. I followed the track to the road. Right would take me back to the city. Left would take me to the border with South Sudan and a three-hundred-and-fifty-mile drive to Burunda.

I saw a figure emerge from the trees and start running toward me. For a moment I felt my hand move toward the Sig under my arm. I stayed it and a moment later Van Hurt scrambled into the passenger seat beside me.

"Is he dead?"

I nodded. "You did OK."

"Gee, thanks, sir. C'mon. Let's get the hell out of here."

I pulled the cell from my pocket. It rang twice and Kuku answered.

"Yes."

"He's dead. Are you at the airport?"

"No."

"I told you to get a ticket and go!"

"This is my home. You know nothing of this place. I have to stay here. There will be war now, and the forces of darkness will win if the good people run. Goodbye, Dash."

"Wait!"

But the line went dead. Van Hurt's face had flushed red and his eyes were bright. "What the hell are you playing at?"

I snarled, "Mind your own damned business. Just give thanks you're still alive!"

The blood drained from his face. I spun the wheel and pulled onto the road, headed south toward the border. We wouldn't go to the border. A couple of miles down the road, according to Van Hurt's instructions, I turned onto a dirt track and we lurched and jolted through the tall grass and the twisted, gnarled tree to an area of flat land. There, a hundred yards distant, in the cover of some low hills, was an unmarked green chopper. Two men in green fatigues stood beside it, watching us. In their hands they had assault rifles and for a moment I wondered if they were going to kill me, but I knew they wouldn't. Otropoco was not done with me. He had at least one more job for me to do. And after that—after that, I knew what I had in store.

After my next job he was going to start torturing Claire, and he was going to force me to witness it until she died.

And then he was going to send me home, to live the rest of my life with that memory. That was Otropoco. That was who he was.

THIRTEEN

NOBODY TROUBLED US OVER SOUTH SUDAN, AND nobody in the chopper spoke. We flew low over savannah that was bordering on desert, with sparse woodlands, scorched grassland and dry, red and yellow sand.

The flight took two hours. The guys with guns ignored us, but occasionally I caught Van Hurt watching me. There was no expression on his face, but his eyes said he was calculating, or trying to think something through.

Finally we crossed into Burunda. Flying low over the jungle we sighted Apodo-Djamu in the distance, over to the west, and shortly after that we saw the camp up ahead of us. We came in to land to the south of the huts, kicking up a windstorm of dust and bowing, tossing trees. A couple of soldiers with rifles came to meet us. They seemed to ignore Van Hurt and me and strolled away with the gunmen from the chopper.

Behind them were a couple of women with bright eyes and no teeth. They spoke to us, gesturing toward the house where I had met Otropoco. When they were done Van Hurt looked at me resentfully and said, "They have lunch ready for us, buffalo stew."

I nodded at the women and smiled, and followed them toward the hut. On the way I turned to Van Hurt.

"All the way here you've been trying to work it out. Let me make it easy for you. Keep your mouth shut, and I'll keep mine shut. You have exactly nothing to lose. I have another job now. When that job is done, he will start torturing my fiancée, and he will force me to witness it. Eventually he will kill her, and then he'll send me back to New York to live with the memories." I gave my head a small twitch, trying to read his face. "You'll be laughing all the way."

A cloud of resentment and anger passed over his face. He drew breath to answer but I shook my head. "Don't. We're being watched. Sneer if you want to, laugh, but show you're on top."

It took him a very long four or five seconds. Then he sneered, gave a small laugh and turned to climb the steps. Shaking his head he muttered, "You are so full of shit."

That made me smile. I didn't know if he was playacting or if he meant it. Maybe it was a bit of both, but it was good enough for my purposes. I followed after him.

On the wooden table on the terrace there two earthenware bowls of dense beef stew, and a large, stone-baked bread. We sat and as we tore bread and started eating, the woman with few teeth brought out a couple of cold beers. She said something and cackled. I smiled at her as I took the beer and Van Hurt spoke into his stew.

"A man has got to eat good meat if he wants to have strong children."

He slumped back in his chair and his eyes said he wasn't enjoying himself. "You got children, Harry?"

I shook my head. "No."

He crossed his arms as he nodded his head. He made a fist with his right hand but laid two fingers across his elbow. I spooned some tender beef into my mouth and tore a piece of bread from the loaf. He said:

"So Claire is the only root you have. Your only Achilles' heel."

"Yeah," I said with my mouth full. "I guess so."

He nodded again, closed his fingers and raised his thumb, like he was agreeing with me. "Fortunately, I've never had the time for kids or women. Free spirit, know what I mean? Answer to no one. Family, loved ones—" He was holding my eye like he had it in a vice. "They're a bind. What's worse, they give a man a hold over you."

"What is this, bonding time? Are we pals now?"

His expression didn't change. It was neutral. He nodded a couple of times imperceptibly, like he was telling me yeah, he had two kids and a wife and he was trying to share that with me. Then he leaned his elbows on the table again and shoveled meat into his mouth.

"You're a miserable bastard, Harry. You know that? I figure, I have always figured, if you go out with a guy and kill someone, that forms a bond, right? You must have felt that with the guys at the SAS—"

"The SAS never held my girlfriend hostage, they never blackmailed me and they *always* give the guys the chance to turn down a mission if they think it is not feasible."

"No shit?"

A wave of frustration and irritation made me snap. "What's your point, Van Hurt? What are you trying to tell me?"

He frowned and gave his head a tiny shake. Then, "Ah, forget it! It's just, if we're going to be working together, we might as well be mates. But if this is how you want it..." He shrugged and trailed off.

I scowled. "Be *working together?* I was told it was two jobs!"

He rolled his eyes and jerked his head toward the glaring dust in the yard. "Here comes his nibs."

I turned and watched the ghastly, mutilated form of Otropoco limping across the dirt. He had on loose cream pants, a white shirt and a cream jacket. There was a scarf across his face and a Panama hat on his head. He arrived at the steps and heaved his way up to drop into a chair. The scarf across his mouth was billowing and dragging into his maw by turns as he gasped for breath. After a moment, when he had started to settle, he asked me, "How long do you think I have to live, Harry?"

I didn't hesitate. "Less than a week."

He wheezed a high-pitched laugh. "You intend to kill me. The doctors give me a full life span, another forty or fifty years. Of course, the longer I live, the more protracted is your pain. The sooner I die, the more intense is your pain. A hard choice for you."

"Yeah." I said it like I was bored.

"Your next job will take you far from here, across the Atlantic, to Washington. The one in the District of Columbia."

"You're sending me to DC? That's risky for you."

"Is it? I don't think so. Tell me where is the risk. I will be kept informed every step of the way. And if the information stops coming in, Claire will be gang raped every day until the communication is restored. Who knows, you might become a daddy."

I could feel the Sig heavy under my arm. The temptation to kill him right there was almost overwhelming. But the risk was too high, and the odds were still stacked in his favor. I didn't blink. I allowed a hint of contempt to creep into my face.

"You fancy yourself as some kind of DC Comics mastermind evil genius. Maybe that's how you deal with this awful thing that has happened to you. But the fact is you're pretty stupid sometimes, Otropoco. You should know that a man is never more out of your control, never more dangerous, than when he loses hope."

"Have you lost hope, Harry?"

I pointed at him across the table. "You are denying me hope. I am a realist, Otropoco, and the training that was drilled into us day after day at the Regiment was based on one, inviolable, golden rule: face reality. Face the reality of the situation you are in. And what you two," I pointed from him to Van Hurt and back again, "what you two keep showing me is that there is nothing I can do. I am going to do one more job and then you are going to rape and torture Claire until she dies, and you are going to make me witness that."

I reached under my arm and pulled the Sig, and pointed it at his head. "So you explain to me, if I pull the trigger right now and blow your brains out, what have I got to lose? To me it looks like you overplayed your hand. There is nothing you are going to do if I disobey you, if I go to the Feds or the CIA with your location, or if I shoot you right now—there is nothing you are going to do in those circumstances that you are not going to do anyway." I put the gun back. "So where is your threat, and where is my incentive to obey you?"

He made a strange rasping noise and his scarf seemed to suck into what was left of his mouth. For a moment I thought he was choking to death and started calculating my run across to Claire's hut. But as he clawed the cloth from his teeth I realized he was laughing.

"It's a good point, but you are a fool if you think I haven't considered it. I have told you that when this second job is concluded, you can both return to your little ranch on Wyoming." A little wheezing laugh turned into a cough.

"I'd have to be some special kind of stupid to believe that, Otropoco, wouldn't I?" He shook his head. "You'd have to be some special kind of smart. You'd have to know me a lot better than you do, and you'd have to know that I think many, many moves in advance. I was, by the way, very impressed by your work in Tubdhaawi. You did very well, considering you were not fully briefed."

"What do you man, I wasn't—"

"Napoleon was under a lot of pressure, not only from the United States, but also from Europe and people close to him, not least your special little friend, Kuku."

"What kind of pressure?"

"To move toward an open democracy, to align itself more with the West, women's rights, a ban on child slavery, universal suffrage, all those things we hold so dear. But of course he had risen to power with the help of the Islamic powers in the country, who were seeking a closer alliance with a Russian-backed Iran."

His one working eye creased into a grin. "I am pleased to say that a very hush-hush offer from the American government had all but secured an agreement whereby American and British companies would start to exploit gold and oil reserves in Tubdhaawi, on a profit-sharing basis, on the condition that Napoleon initiated a program of social and political reform."

I felt a cold rage well up inside me and struggled to control my voice and my actions. My voice was barely a whisper. "That's why you had me kill him? Because he was going to bring democracy to the country?"

"Oh no, not at all. I have no interest in politics, Harry. I had you kill him because now the country will slide into civil war, I will sell guns to the jihadists—in fact I have already sold guns to the jihadists—and in exchange for this excellent assassination I will receive stakes in the gold mines and the oil." He seemed to smile again. "I mean, you have to forgive me, Harry. You stole almost everything I had. I have a lot of catching up to do."

I didn't say anything. I was afraid if I did or said anything I would kill him right there and then. He watched me in silence for a moment. Then slowly removed the scarf to show the grotesque monstrosity that was his face.

"Look at me, Harry. My body is a reflection of the ugliness inside. I understand you pleaded with the lovely Kuku to flee to America or Britain. But of course she was far too devoted to her country and her people to agree to that."

It was deliberate and obvious, and he waited for me to ask, "Was? *Was* far too devoted to her country and her people?"

"She was executed while you were flying off South Sudan. She was deemed part of the old regime, a Western sympathizer. You know all the labels they invent to justify murdering people."

I fought for a moment to suppress the tears. "She was beautiful, noble and intelligent, ad you had her murdered."

In that moment, his lipless leer was the ugliest thing I had ever seen in my life. He nodded. "I'd say that was a pretty accurate assessment of the situation. As to your incentives, I would say it's like this. Obey me, and I will deliver you back to Wyoming with ninety-nine percent of the damage on the inside. Disobey me or cause me problems, and I will deliver you back to Wyoming with you your healthy, handsome self, and Claire looking pretty much like me. Is that incentive enough?"

A wave of nausea swept over me. I said, "Yes, Otropoco, that is incentive enough,"

"Good, good, then let me fill you in on the broad outline, and then Van Hurt will give you the finer details. What you are going to do is to hijack an airliner flying from Burunda to Washington DC." He threw back his head and shrieked with laughter. "And you will make full use—*full use*, Harry—of the diplomatic bag!"

FOURTEEN

HE SENT ONE OF THE WOMEN TO GO GET SOME GIN AND tonics. Van Hurt set about building three tall glasses of ice, lime, Beefeater and tonic, handed them out and sat watching me with no expression on his face, while Otropoco rattled his glass against his exposed teeth and spilled half his drink out the side of his mouth and down his chin.

"What," he asked, as he wiped his chin with his handkerchief, "would you say, Harry, is the great advantage of a criminal economy?"

I shrugged, sighed and shook my head to let him know I was bored. "You don't pay tax."

He made a horrible noise in his throat that wanted to be a laugh. "That is definitely one of them, but the big advantage is that it is a stable economy. Whatever stupidity the politicians get up to, raising tax and interest rates, playing with corporation tax, value added tax, carbon tax, fucking sneezing tax—none of that affects you. You are immune from the vagaries of the market. The only risk you face is the possibility of some bastard who is bigger and badder than you coming and stealing your market."

"That's fascinating. As soon as I get home to New York I will immediately invest all my money in the Sinaloa Cartel. They were bigger and badder than you in the Gulf Cartel, weren't they?"

He nodded. "Of course, they had the help of the CIA and the American military. But here is the really interesting thing. Big economies, where billions of dollars move every day, like the United States economy or the EU economy, these economies are crippled by regulation and control. Smaller economies, third world economies, are more relaxed, less regulated, easier to work with."

"Right, I guess so. Otropoco, I know you are not a man who wastes time or words. I know you're having fun building up to something."

He rattled his drink on his teeth and spilt a bit more over his tongue. While he mopped it up he said, "You have somewhere you need to be?"

"You tell me. You said something about Washington DC."

"DC, yeah, capital of the world. Do you think, Harry, if the American economy collapsed overnight, would it affect the European economy?"

"You know damned well, Otropoco, it would bring down the whole of the Western economy. What's your point?"

"Yes, but it would not bring down *my economy!*" He had turned suddenly savage and thumped his chest with his thumb. "You can play bored, patronizing, talking to me like I am stupid or crazy, but when Americans and Europeans and Japanese are eating food in the gutters, *my economy is not affected!*"

He was wheezing badly through his open mouth. He looked away and with shaking hands he tied the scarf around his face. I watched it billow in and out until he had calmed down.

"So your job, Harry Bauer," he said, and you could almost smell the green venom on his tongue, "is to cripple the economy of the West."

"We're going to try this again?"

"It should pose a very interesting problem for you. Let me explain to you what I am ordering you to do, and then what I expect you to do. Because I do not believe you have the *cojones* to carry out my orders. If you do, then you can take your darling Claire, physically unhurt, and go anywhere you like in the world."

I was getting anxious and mad, and I had a sick hollow in my gut. "Cut to the chase. What do I have to do?"

"My dear friend, Colonel Alexandrina Vitsin, head of the Special Covert Operations Unit in Moscow, has sent me, via Iran, a very special rucksack."

He paused, watching me. My skin went cold and I felt the hairs on the back of my neck prickle.

"A tactical nuclear device."

"That's correct. In the late '90s they had a yield of one kiloton. Ample for our needs, but the one we have is a later generation and it has a yield of almost two kilotons. Detonated over the White House or the Capitol, it will vaporize everything in a mile radius. Within minutes the winds caused by the blast will carry the radiation across Virginia, West Virginia and Pennsylvania; and of course the prevailing winds, assisted by the blast, will carry it very quickly into New Jersey and New York. The United States Government and administration, and the world's most important marketplace in one fell swoop." He made a grotesque cackling sound in his throat. "How long, Harry, after Wall Street and the New York Stock Exchange have imploded, how long before the London Stock Exchange, Brussels and Tokyo collapse?"

I didn't answer. There was no answer. I looked out at the scorching dust. For a few seconds I was overwhelmed by a sense of hopelessness. Otropoco was shaking his head.

"It is essential, on so many levels, symbolic, emotional and practical, that it is detonated over the White House or the Capitol." He considered me a moment and went on. "I know. I know you can't bring yourself to do it. As the evil Han says to John Saxon in *Enter the Dragon*, there is a point beyond which most men will not go. This is something you cannot bring yourself to do. You must turn away, and say, 'No!'"

I still said nothing. I watched his skinny shoulders shake in silence.

"So, if you don't do it, what must you face? This is the art, Harry, the true art of torture. Because what you face if you don't do it, is equally impossible for you to bear. Look at me—"

He removed his Panama hat and his scarf.

"See my nose, torn from my face by a piece of burning timber in the blast. My eye. I will never forget the skin on my face burning as I jumped into the sea to quench the flames. My lips were burned away. Even my teeth were charred. And my right leg, partly torn off by the explosion, was later tidied up in the operating theater. Look at me, and absorb what you see. Because you will remain the handsome, male animal you are today. But she—" He pointed across the dust to Claire's cabin. "She will be gang raped every day by my men until she begs to die. You will watch. And when she begs to die I, personally, will do this to her." He gestured at himself with both hands. "Then, and only then, will I give her back to you, so that you can love her and care for her for the rest of your life, *knowing* that you did that to her." It was hard to tell if he was grinning. He was always grinning. But his one working eye said he was amused. "As I said, Harry, an interesting problem for you."

"There is no problem," I told him. "I'll take the bomb. But how can I be sure you won't do that to her anyway? What's my guarantee you'll let her go?"

"Come, Harry! What guarantee could I possibly give you that you would believe?"

"Let me think about it?"

"Don't think too long. I'll want an answer by tonight. Your plane flies tomorrow night."

He got to his feet with difficulty, struggled down the steps and limped across the dusty square toward his hut. When he was gone I turned my eyes on Van Hurt.

"You knew about this?"

"Of course. And so did you. You told me. You just didn't

know the details. What did you think, that he was going to make some careless mistake, you were going to beat everybody up and ride off into the sunset? C'mon, Harry. He's got you and you know it."

I stared at him for a long moment. "What game are you playing, Van Hurt? What's in this for you?"

His face went tight with anger, he even lost a little color as he leaned forward with his elbows on the table and said, "You are a very stupid man, sometimes, Harry. I am just-doing-my-job!"

He stared at me for a moment too long and stood. "Come on, let's go inside and I'll brief you. I know you well enough by now to know you will take the job."

I watched him from my chair. "What makes you think that?"

He raised a thumb. "First, you will always take a chance, however small, in a hopeless situation." He raised his index. "Second, you will never give up without a fight," he raised his middle finger, "Third, you always do what you say you're going to do."

I followed him inside and dropped into one of the wicker armchairs while he went for his file. He brought it over and dropped it on the coffee table.

"I had a friend once—"

"Are you sure?"

"Just shut the fuck up for five minutes, will you, Harry?" He sat down. "He was a Brit working-class kid who'd started forging a career in the army. He gave me some advice once. I took it to heart and I am going to pass it on to you. You can do what you like with it." I waited. After a moment he said, "I was young, a bit of an asshole, thought I knew everything, had all the answers, a bit like you. and one day Bert says to me, 'Chris,' he says, 'don't be a cunt all your life.'"

"Thanks."

"Yeah, you're welcome. You know? It's OK to stop at some point."

"I get it."

He opened the folder and extracted a US passport. He handed

it to me. I was Lt. Edward Vandenberg of the United States Air Force. I had been seconded to Burunda to train pilots in the Burunda Air Force. I was stationed at Wright Patterson AFB and lived in Dayton, Ohio, with my wife, Claire, and two kids, Harry and Maria.

I nodded. "That's funny. You have a sense of humor. I thought you'd stopped being a c—"

"I didn't pick the names or the backstory. Ease up, will you?"

He tossed a leather wallet at me. "Credit cards, two thousand dollars, photographs et cetera."

I opened it and leafed through. There was a picture of me and Claire outside my ranch. We had two kids with us, a boy and a girl. It was obviously photoshopped, but it was well done and credible.

He tossed me a ticket.

"This is a Burunda Airlines flight direct to Washington DC. You will board with diplomatic immunity from the Burunda government, and you will use the diplomatic bag for your luggage. You will have three cases. Two will be filled with clothes, the third will carry the nuclear device. In addition, you will have an attaché case. Your instructions are as follows. You will do nothing until you are twenty minutes from DC. Then you will open your attaché case and extract a Smith and Wesson 500. You are familiar with it?"

"Yeah, I'm familiar with it. It's a fifty-caliber cannon that blows holes through concrete walls."

"Exactly. You will go to the pilots' cabin and blow out the lock. Kill the pilot and the copilot and anybody else you need to eliminate. Depressurize the cabins and come in low over either the White House or the Capitol. Either one will do."

I frowned. "And then?"

He shrugged. "Otropoco's instructions are for you to take a parachute and jump once the plane is locked on course. Of course, the problem with that is that you'd have to stay with it long enough to avoid it being intercepted or shot down." He hesitated. "I have a suggestion."

I shook my head. "I do not fix a collision course with the White House. I drop to about one thousand four or five hundred feet a mile or so out to see and set a course for Mount Airy or Hapsburg. That is going to take me up the Potomac and right over DC.

"As soon as I am at one thousand five hundred feet I call Air Traffic Control and report a Burunda Airlines flight in distress. I am trying to maintain altitude but I need to land somewhere north of Silver Spring. That guarantees they don't shoot me down. We are now a couple of minutes outside DC, at most. I am going to steer a course halfway between the White House and the Capitol, right over the roof of FBI headquarters on Pennsylvania Avenue. That is where the bomb should detonate. How do I do that?"

"We'll be tracking the plane by satellite. We'll detonate it. You need to bail out as soon as you have radioed for help, as far from the blast as possible. You want to head toward the Carolinas, or Florida."

"Then I get arrested and die in prison while he tortures Claire to death."

"What's your alternative?" I drew breath but he put his finger to his lips and glanced at the lamp above our heads. "Look, in five minutes that you've had the plan you have improved it to a point where you have one chance in a hundred. It's a damned sight better than the zero chance you had before. Spend some time on it, think if there is a way you can guarantee Claire's release and safety, and her return to the States, or Europe."

I let him see all the suspicion and loathing in my eyes. He shook his head, glanced at the lamp and leaned toward me.

"I am just trying to do my job." He stood. "I'm going to get things ready. You need anything, you need to discuss anything, give me a shout. Otherwise we reconvene here at nine PM to finalize details and confirm to Otropoco that you've made your choice."

He held my eye a moment, then turned and left.

Was the son of a bitch really trying to help me, or was he just part of Otropoco's mind games? I went and sat and looked through the anemic file again. There was practically nothing in it. Because it was a suicide mission. The bomb would be in the hold. They would detonate it, and all I had to do was get on the plane and jump off into the radioactive Atlantic.

I remembered the Jewish guy haranguing God—"We had a deal!" and God telling him, "I sent you a warning, a dingy, a rowing boat and a helicopter! What more do you want?"—and decided to suspend judgment until I had more data. Where I needed to focus my attention now was on the plan. I had to analyze it from that very moment, where I was looking at the photograph of Claire and our future kids, through the jungle to Al-Islamabad and the airport, onto the plane and all the way across Africa and the Atlantic Ocean. I had to study the whole, damned trajectory. I felt the Sig still under my arm and asked myself, "Where? Where do you get off, Harry?"

FIFTEEN

I wasn't getting very far. I was sitting on the wooden veranda drinking a cold beer, going over the route for the thousandth time, thinking about every moment and every transition, looking for a moment I could seize to make a move. The risk factor for Claire was too high at every step, and I was reaching desperation point where I knew I would have to do something, anything, whatever the risk might be. The one thing I could not do was nothing.

Then, for a moment, I was suddenly aware that something had changed. I listened. There was only silence and I realized that was it. There had always been a generator humming in the background. It must have been in a hut somewhere because it was quiet. But now it had stopped I had noticed it.

And then there were voices, shouts, men barking orders. I went out to the veranda. I saw four soldiers dressed in khaki carrying assault rifles running toward Claire's hut. Adrenaline lurched in my belly and my hand moved to my Sig under my arm. But they didn't go in. They surrounded the door, two on their knees and two standing, training their weapons out at the square.

There were other men too, streaming this way and that, racing to the entrances to the village in Jeeps and on foot. I saw

Otropoco leaning on his doorjamb, looking out, looking at me, and Van Hurt running toward my hut with his gun in his hand. He bounded up the steps and shoved the gun in my face. His eyes were crazy and his teeth were clenched.

"*What have you done, you goddamn fool?*"

I started to say, "You better get that weapon out of my face before I—"

He didn't let me finish. He grabbed my collar and pushed me back, hissing under his breath, "I screwed the generator and we only have a few minutes till they fix it. Shut up and listen!"

He shoved me into a chair and stood over me.

"As long as the generator is out the bugs don't work. We are on the clock. I have been trying to tell you, you stupid fuck, that I want to help you. You *cannot* do this alone and you have nothing to lose by working with me. Whether you believe it or not, I work for the South African NIA, and I *need* to get this intel to them before it's too late."

"No."

"*What?*"

"You inform the NIA, they inform Washington and Otropoco kills Claire."

"We are talking about millions of lives!"

"There has to be another way."

There were shouts outside. He swallowed hard. "Jesus!" He stepped forward and delivered a stinging backhander across my face, then bellowed at the top of his voice, "*Did you disable the generator?*"

I scowled at him. "God damn it, Van Hurt!"

"Yeah, you owe me that and a lot more. Is there anyone, any colleague or department, *anyone* we can contact who can neutralize the bomb without jeopardizing Claire? Who could organize a raid on the camp to release her?"

I shook my head. Voices shouting, coming closer.

"*For God's sake, Harry!*"

"How do you figure it?"

He spoke fast. "Tomorrow, on the way to town, we make a detour, make the call, they raid the camp, seize the tracking device and the detonator and free Claire. You must have people you know or whom you've worked with!"

Deep, guttural voices behind him and two large men in khaki climbed the steps. They spoke in a local language I didn't understand.

I said, "Yes, OK."

He spoke to the men behind him without turning around and pistol-whipped me across the face.

"Try something like that again and you'll have the pleasure of watching these guys having a little party with Mrs. Bauer!"

I touched the warm trickle of blood from my cheek and licked it off my fingers. I held Van Hurt's eyes for a count of three and said quietly, "You really don't want that to happen, Van Hurt. I do believe I have nothing to lose."

He smiled. It wasn't a nice thing to see. "Just keep your hair on, Bauer, and don't do anything stupid. It'll all work out in the end." Then he pointed at me in the face. "I owed you. Now we're even."

I didn't answer. I watched him and the two gorillas leave the hut. He'd left me with the Sig again. I walked out to the veranda just in time to see Otropoco withdrawing inside again.

Van Hurt was right about one thing. I was about as screwed as a cheap whore during shore leave. If he was South African NIA he might just help. If he wasn't, I was no more screwed than I was before. There was also the question of what would he and Otropoco stand to gain from pretending he was NIA?

Maybe nothing, maybe something. Maybe it was a simple, sadistic mind game. Or maybe it was a deeper game. It would not pay to underestimate Otropoco.

Nothing much happened for the rest of the day and next morning, at seven AM Van Hurt was at my door in a Land Rover. The sun wasn't up yet, but the sky was a pale gray and the birds were going crazy, getting out of bed and making breakfast. He had three suitcases in the back, and one of them I knew was the bomb. I chucked in my own hold-all on top and climbed in.

If you have never driven a Land Rover through the jungle with a two megaton tactical nuclear device in the trunk, you haven't really lived. Still, having said that, it's not something I would recommend. Maybe have oysters and a two-thousand-dollar bottle of champagne in Venice instead.

We followed the same route as before, passed the same village and waved, and eventually came out of the forest and onto the main highway at the medium-sized town of Digbo. Here, instead of continuing toward Apodo-Djamu, he came off the highway and onto the smaller road that led into the town. We hadn't spoken since we'd got into the truck, but now he glanced at me and put his finger to his lips.

We passed the standard shantytown suburbs, but as we approached the center of town, where there were actual houses with gardens, shops and apartment blocks, on the right-hand side he pointed to a sprawling shopping mall. Here we turned in, found a place to park, and he killed the engine.

"I'm going to get some coffee." He gave his head a jerk to say I should go with him.

He swung down and I followed. The parking lot was practically empty and he walked slowly, pulling a crumpled pack of Camels from his pocket. He poked a cigarette in his mouth, paused to light it and inhaled deeply. As he started to walk again he said, "Here's how it goes down."

"Let's hear it. I'll tell you if it goes down that way or not."

He ignored me. "We buy a burner. You call your people, warn them about the bomb. Then I call my people and we call in a raid on the camp."

"No."

He stopped, faced me and stared at me, and in that moment I knew he was what he said he was. He was South African Intelligence. It was writ large in the terror on his face.

"Are you out of your mind? What's the matter with you?"

"Give me a backhander and shove me toward the shop. Keep walking, we might be being watched."

He didn't hold back. He gave me a hefty slap and shoved me toward the shop. He used that as an excuse to look around and we went through the sliding doors into the mall. The shops were just opening and there was no one around. Asa we walked I asked him, "Is the truck bugged?"

"Probably."

"OK, now listen carefully. This is something you have to understand. Maybe you are NIA. Probably you are. But if we alert Washington that there is a tactical nuclear device on board this flight they are going to ground the flight. They are not going to let it anywhere near DC. You can bet your life Otropoco has people at the airport here, and probably among the cops too, if not in the government itself. He will be monitoring this flight and the minute it is delayed he will go into a rage and he will put Claire through every kind of hell. I am not going to let that happen."

He stopped again and turned to face me. He looked sick. "Harry, you have to think this through—"

"Don't even try, Van Hurt."

"Millions of people are going to die. Do you understand that? I have been under cover with this bastard for six months. I know what he is capable of. Millions, Harry, *millions* of people, and at least half of them from radiation sickness."

"Stop."

"And that is just the start of it. Have you thought through the long-term impact, when the stock market collapses?"

"Chris!" Using his first name made him stop and listen. "Listen to me. You can't be doing this. You are drawing attention to us and you are putting everything at risk. You have to accept that I am not going to alert Washington, and neither are you. If you try, I'll kill you. We have to find another way. Let's go have coffee."

I turned and walked away from him toward the big supermarket. There the broad passage made a dogleg and down on the right there was a café. I went and leaned on the counter and told the girl to give me two double espressos and four croissants. Behind me I heard a chair scrape and knew Van Hurt had followed and sat down. I joined him at the table. He looked about as mad as a man can get without reaching for his axe.

"Do that to me again," he said quietly, "and I will shoot you where you stand."

"A lot of people have tried, Van Hurt. Believe me, you won't be the first to achieve it. Now, we have a problem and we need to solve it. If we work together we stand a better chance. But we have a red line here, and that red line is Claire."

"One woman." He nodded a few times, a little too fast. "*One* woman is your red line because you want to—" He bit back the words he was going to say and instead went with, "*marry* her. But you don't draw any red lines for the *millions* of men, women and children who could die if that case reaches Washington."

"I didn't say that. That is a red line we are both agreed on. But you are willing to sacrifice my wife to save those people, and I am not."

He rubbed his face with his hands, then placed them in front of his nose and mouth, like he was praying.

"There are five and a half million people in the DC metropolitan area. Almost a million in the city center."

"There is nothing you are going to tell me this morning that I haven't been over a hundred times during the night. But I am going to tell you something. Otropoco was right. There are certain points a person will not go beyond. And I will not—I *cannot*—do that to Claire. So let's stop wasting time. You have a choice. You go solo and try to warn the US Embassy or the Feds, or you work with me and we try to find another way."

"What '*other way*'? If you don't get on that plane, that in itself will trigger an alert. And if you do get on the plane, what the hell can you do anyway?"

"The suitcases have to go on."

"*What?*"

The girl came with our coffee and croissants. She told us what she'd brought, "Two double espresso for you, and four croissants." She gave me a big smile and went away. Van Hurt said, "Are you completely out of your mind?"

"Just calm down, will you? Keep going like this and the whole thing will be academic."

"He-has-the-detonator!"

"I know. Now let's put this to rest. If we alert Washington he will find out about it. If you alert your people and call in an attack on the compound, they will alert Washington and he will find out about it. Washington cannot know. That is final and I am not going to waste any more time discussing it."

His face flushed. "So what the *fuck* do we do?"

"First, you get a grip. Second, I check in and we load the suitcases onto the plane. Then we go back and kill Otropoco."

He made a big, "Ha!" sound. Then he leaned back in his chair, threw his head back and laughed out loud. I sipped my coffee and ate half a croissant while I waited for him to finish.

"You are *out-of-your-mind!* There are a hundred men there. Half of them are mercenaries, vets from God knows how many African campaigns. These are hard, brutal professionals."

"Enough, Van Hurt. I don't want another negative word out of your mouth. I kept enough C4 from Tubdhaawi to create a decent diversion and take out a significant number of the mercenaries. If the bang is big enough the government troops will run. We can pick up a couple of assault rifles from the camp. I've done this kind of operation a hundred times. You just have to stay cool and do it right."

He looked away, his lips clamped tight. He didn't say a negative word. His face said them all for him.

He lifted both hands, still not looking at me. "This is not being negative. I am just covering the angles. What happens if we get to the camp and a stray bullet, a lucky shot—hell! Otropoco lets you know he has her with a gun to her head. Put down your weapons or else. What happens then to the suitcase?"

"I have that covered."

"Oh, great! You have that covered."

"We remove the bomb from the suitcase before checking it in."

"Are you—? You just!" He put both hands to his head. "You just get more fucking crazy with every word you utter!"

"Stop getting your pink frillies in a tangle, will you! I make a call."

"Now you make a call."

I gave a single nod. "I make a call to somebody I know and I tell them where the bomb is. They send an expert to disarm it."

"Jesus Christ!"

I scowled at him. "Well what's the big difference, Van Hurt? If we notify Washington, what are they going to do, fire the damn thing to the moon? They'll send a team to disarm it. This is the same thing and probably the same team. Only this way Otropoco is not alerted and the flight goes ahead as planned."

"What about when you don't get on the plane, won't he be alerted?"

"By that time we'll be knocking on his door at the camp."

"Who are you going to call?"

"That's something you don't need to know. Let's go get that burner."

SIXTEEN

We made our way into the supermarket and I bought two Chinese cell phones off a hook on a rack. I put ten bucks on each of them at the checkout and we walked back out to the parking lot. As we were crossing toward the truck he said suddenly, "You've really got me freaking out about this. How long is it going to take them to get a team here?"

I turned to face him. "Less time than it takes to fly Burunda Airlines to DC. And in any case the flight doesn't leave till this evening. What's the matter with you?"

For a moment he seemed speechless. "It's just the timing is so tight. You seem like you haven't got a problem in the world. Shouldn't you be calling them already? They have to assemble a team of experts and get them to the arsehole of the world in just a few hours." I stared at him. He pointed to the truck. "You can't call from there."

I narrowed my eyes. "Do you think it might be a good idea if when I call them I tell them where the bomb is?"

He made several false starts, then nodded. "Yeah, yeah, OK, sorry."

"If you don't calm down I'm going to sheet you."

He sighed and closed his eyes. "OK, I'm sorry."

"I'm not joking." He opened his eyes and I held his gaze. His face went gray. "There is too much riding on this. Get a grip or I'll shoot you stone dead."

"OK."

I drove. We returned to the main highway and plunged back into deep rainforest. I drove slowly, scanning the sides of the roads for some kind of path or clearing. I found it after about a mile and a half. The trees receded from the side of the road and there was a narrow track, probably used by shepherds to guide their goats and sheep.

I turned off and I crawled along, with branches brushing the sides of the truck and snapping as we pushed forward. Finally we came to a small clearing. I stopped and killed the engine. I swung down and we stood listening. There was not a sound.

"Look around."

We spent fifteen or twenty minutes scouting out the surrounding area and found nothing. So we made tracks into the undergrowth, dragging the heaviest of the three cases with us. When we had reached a suitable spot I dropped the case and opened it. All there was inside was a steel tube about nineteen inches long, lying diagonally across the case in a molded, foam housing. It was about six inches in diameter. In the side there was a small LED display with two very small bulbs beside it. At that moment the display said nothing and the lights were off.

I took a photograph of it with the phone and we started digging. When we were about three feet deep I laid the canister in and covered it with dirt. Over the dirt I laid leaves, dead branches and stones. Then I stood and dialed a number. It rang a couple of times before it was answered.

"Sir? It's Harry... Yeah, I didn't think I'd be calling so soon either. I have to be very brief. In a moment I am going to send you a photograph along with my GPS location. The photograph is of a TND...yes sir, a nuclear device. We need a team here yesterday to deactivate it." I was quiet for a moment, then said, "I am in Burunda, sir, and this is very, very urgent because the bomb will be remotely detonated in about fourteen or fifteen hours. I can't explain anything right now, sir. We need to act."

I hung up and went to send the photograph and my location. The distinctive click made me stop.

"Give me the phone, Harry."

I turned to face him. He was just out of reach. The gun was pointing at my chest, where he couldn't miss, and his hand was not shaking. I said:

"Why don't you come and get it?"

He smiled without much humor. "Otropoco might want you alive. Personally, I don't give a shit and I am quite happy to shoot you right here. His motivation is revenge and hatred and all that shit you get to carry when you lose half your face. Me? I want the money. And the money comes from knowing just who Harry Bauer works for. There are *a lot* of people asking that question, Harry, and they are prepared to pay big bucks to find out. And now, your employer's number is on that phone. So, Harry, give me the phone."

I laughed. "You think you can trace my employer from the call I just made?"

"No, Harry, but I know a man in Moscow who can, and another one in Beijing. The conversation is over. Give me the phone or I will shoot you."

"What about the bomb and the flight to DC? What are you going to tell—"

"Not a problem, Harry. I know a dozen guys who will fly to DC for a thousand bucks, no questions asked. So it explodes over Dulles instead of the White House. Who gives a shit except the crazy Otropoco? Now *give me the phone*."

I handed it over. "If you have no loyalty to Otropoco, let me go back and kill him. Whatever shit you and I may be carrying, Claire doesn't deserve this."

He actually seemed to consider it for a moment. Then he jerked his head at the loose dirt where I had buried the bomb. "Dig it up. I'll think about it while you dig."

I got down on my knees and took two large handfuls of earth. I dumped them to one side and as I took up another two handfuls I said, "She's a doctor. You know that?"

"Yeah." He chuckled. "Don't try and appeal to my better nature, Harry. I haven't got one. I am the lowest kind of sociopathic rat. I will play any part you want me to, and convince you it's for real. But pay me a grand to shoot a schoolgirl in the head and I'll do it without blinking. So don't waste your breath, mate. Just dig."

I was about six inches down by now. I looked up at him and told him, "I'm a very rich man. You know that?"

He grinned. "Yeah, I heard, you stole most of Otropoco's ill-gotten gains."

I nodded as I dumped another load of dirt beside me. "It went into nine figures and the bulk of it is between Panama and Belize. You think we can make a deal?" I settled on my haunches with two handfuls of dirt and stones. "We go to an internet café. I make a transfer. The deal is, in exchange you disappear with my phone and you let me go ahead with the plan as was."

"How much?"

"A hundred million bucks."

He laughed. "You're kidding!"

"I am not kidding. I'll give you a hundred and fifty if you'll agree right now."

He was gaping. Gaping is what stupid people do. The dirt went straight in his eyes. From the squatting position I jumped forward across the hole and came at him from his left as he screamed and fired wildly at where I had been. He got off two rounds before I smashed my fist into the base of his skull. He grunted and staggered. I levered the weapon out of his fingers, marched him ten paces into the undergrowth, hooked my right arm around his throat and my left around the back of his neck, and choked the life out of him. Just to make sure, when I dropped him to the ground I stamped on the back of his neck.

Otropoco had taught me to be careful.

I retrieved the cell from his pocket. All it would have led him to was my answering machine in Manhattan. He had been just a little too eager for me to make the call, and the day before he had been just a little too eager to know who I worked for.

Now I pulled out the second burner and made the call.

"Sir, it's Harry."

"Harry, how are you? I didn't expect—"

"I'm sorry, sir. I need to cut to the chase. I am standing on a two megaton tactical nuclear device in the rainforest in Burunda. I need you to get a team here yesterday. If things go badly, this device will be detonated by remote detonator in about sixteen hours."

"I see—"

You gotta love the Brits. "I am going to send you a photograph of the device and my location. Then I am going to bury the phone under a few inches of soil, with the device so you can access its GPS."

"Splendid. Our nearest qualified troops are in Manda Bay, in Kenya they'll take at least a couple of hours to get there. They won't be able to disarm it, but they should be able to extract it and contain it so that no electronic signals can reach it. Meanwhile..."

"Sir, that sounds like a plan. I have to move. I have some people I need to see."

"You can update me when you get back."

"I will, sir."

I hung up, sent him the photograph and location from the other phone, and buried it, wrapped in a plastic food wrapper I found in the truck, a few inches under the soil. I covered it again with leaves and twigs and headed back to the Land Rover.

I climbed in behind the wheel and sat thinking. I had to act fast. The first thing I had to do was to check the cases onto the plane through the diplomatic pouch. That might prove tricky without Van Hurt, but I'd have to muddle through. That done, I had to get back to the camp without raising the alarm, and without being seen.

And that was the easy bit. After that, only the devil knew what I was going to do. And he wasn't telling. All I could do was go one step at a time, and make sure each step was taken well.

I marked my location on the phone I had kept, found my way back to the highway and floored the pedal all the way to Burunda International Airport, just outside Apodo-Djamu. As I approached I slowed to a moderate speed, pulled into the parking lot and parked as close to the airport entrance as I could. I took a couple of minutes to cool down and center my thoughts. A glance in the mirror told me my appearance needed attention. I looked a wreck.

The airport was a small, one-story affair with the name BURUNDA standing in big blue letters over the entrance. There were not many people in the main hall, and fewer cops. I found the johns, slipped in and scrubbed my hands and face, straightened my shirt and ran wet fingers through my hair. I didn't look great, but I told myself I looked windswept and interesting. That would have to do.

I pushed out of the john and crossed the tiled concourse to the information desk. A pretty girl with very white teeth and enough lipstick to paint your house crimson smiled at me and tilted her head on one side. I leaned on the counter and spoke softly, like it was just between me and her.

"I'm booked on the flight to Washington DC this evening. I'm flying first class and my baggage, three suitcases, is going in the diplomatic pouch. My assistant usually takes care of these things, but he had to attend to some urgent—"

"May I see your passport and your reservation?"

I slid them across to her. She examined them and typed at a computer which was extremely advanced and sophisticated in the '90s.

"Yes, here you are!" she said and beamed at me. "I'll just call Mr. Deng, and he will take care of you."

Mr. Deng took no time at all to appear. He came out of a door across the hall in gray pants and a blue, double-breasted blazer and hurried across the floor toward me. I smiled and shook his hand and he, while he shook, looked anxiously around me.

"Lieutenant Vandenberg." He pronounced it the English way, *leftenant*. "Such a pleasure, thank you, good morning. I, I, I..."

I guess he decided he couldn't say "I" anymore because he stopped and looked around me. I made my smile a reassuring one.

"You are wondering where Mr. Van Hurt is?"

"I was told," he bent both his knees when he said *was*, "I *was* told that Mr. Van Hurt would be taking care of everything."

I chuckled, put my hand on his shoulder and shared the joke with him.

"That is just it, Mr. Deng, he *is* taking care of everything! You know Chris?"

He shrugged. "In passing, from time to time..."

He didn't know Chris. "That man never stops. He is always organizing something. Now he is arranging a farewell lunch for me. Man, my visit to this country has been truly amazing. You guys, I mean it. Amazing. So Chris has arranged something in some fancy restaurant, which is great, but of course it means *I* have to take care of the check-in!"

Deng laughed. It was a weird mechanical laugh with no feeling at all. When he stopped he said, "So where is Mr. Van Hurt?"

"Well, that's what I am telling you. I don't know. He is arranging lunch for me and some friends, a farewell. It's supposed to be a surprise."

He spread his hands. "It is not... It's not—and the cases? There are supposed to be cases."

I let the smile slip from my face. "Is there a problem, Mr. Deng? I was assured there would be no problem. All I am trying to do is check in some suitcases while my assistant arranges lunch. The cases are in my truck."

He wasn't listening to me. He was flapping and he was going to cause me a problem.

"I think perhaps security?" He glanced at the pretty girl with the lipstick. She looked away. "Perhaps I should—"

I stepped forward and gently placed my fingers on his chest. "Mr. Deng? You need to listen to me. Me and my suitcases are covered by diplomatic immunity. You understand that? I was having cocktails with President Majok last night and he personally guaranteed me that status." I gave him a particularly dangerous smile. "You understand, Mr. Deng, that I am personally charged with transporting gifts from the president to friends in the States, in the diplomatic pouch."

He swallowed hard. "I am supposed to speak with Mr. Van Hurt. Where is he?"

I leaned real close to him. "Why don't you ask the president?"

He turned real queasy. I reached in my pocket and pulled out my wallet. I extracted a hundred bucks and slipped it to him. "If it's your payment your worried about, we'll both be back after lunch and he'll take care of you. Now get me someone to load the damn cases, will you?"

He stuffed the money in his pocket and hurried away. I noticed he always walked with his elbows bent and wondered absently why that made people feel more important. He pushed back in through his door and came out two minutes later with four men in khaki shorts and knee socks. They also had khaki shirts, caps and guns. I had a very hot burn in my belly as I watched them approach.

Deng stopped in front of me and gestured to the man on his right.

"Lt. Vandenberg, this is Captain Choi of the Special Airport Police."

I nodded to him. "How do?"

He nodded. "Please, Lt. Vandenberg, show us where the cases are, we will check them into the diplomatic pouch and ensure that they are safe and secure. When you return with Mr. Van Hurt, you will please ask him to report to me or to Mr. Deng."

"No worries. Follow me."

SEVENTEEN

THEY BROUGHT A TROLLEY AND THE FOUR OF THEM
wheeled my three suitcases away across the parking lot and into
the airport, well guarded and secure. One of the guys was about to
grab hold of my sports bag with eight pounds of C4 in it. I told
him I'd be using that later on. He could leave it.

I drove out of the parking lot at a sedate pace and turned
toward the city. I passed the shantytowns, the barefoot kids
playing football and the families squatting among trash staring at
the passing traffic.

I came to the suburbs and slowed, cruising among the streets,
scanning the roadsides for what I needed. What I needed was a
Toyota truck, or something similar. Something as tough as boiled
leather which was completely anonymous. Something you could
drive through a bombing raid with, that nobody would look
twice at. A Toyota truck.

Finally I found one. It's not all that hard, especially in Africa.
It was parked in the road outside an open, iron gate. There was a
kid in plastic flip-flops and Bermuda jeans washing it. I pulled up
across the road from him.

"Hey, kid!" He looked up. "Come over a second."

He looked up and down the road, saw I was alone and approached.

"Yeah?"

I jerked my head at his truck. "You want to sell your Toyota?"

He smiled and shook his head. "No."

"Hear me out. It's a good deal. You get my Land Rover and five hundred American dollars."

His jaw dropped. His eyes opened wide and he laughed. "You must be joking, man."

I raised a finger. "But no questions asked."

I pulled out my wallet and extracted five hundred bucks which I held out to him. "Anybody asks, you came out and your truck was gone, this one was left in its place."

"I dunno, man. Am I gonna get into trouble?"

I was about to answer when I heard a siren blare once. The kid looked away, behind me and I looked in my wing mirror. It was a couple of cops in a jeep. I looked at the kid. He was shaking his head saying, "I don't wanna know, man. I'm sorry..."

I said, "Go inside. You don't want to see this."

The Jeep pulled up just behind me and two cops climbed out. These weren't in khaki. These were in dark blue and had peaked, military-style caps. They also had sidearms and truncheons. They strolled up, one headed for each window. I didn't want that so I opened the door and climbed out, smiling.

"Good afternoon, Officers. How can I—"

The cop on my side, a big guy with two chins and no hair, was backing up and reaching for his gun while the one on the other side, a skinny guy with whiskers and a moustache was scampering to get back to this side. I raised my hands.

"I am sorry! What seems to be the problem?"

"What are you doing here? Why are you talking to that boy? Are you selling drugs?"

I laughed. "No! I am a lieutenant in the American Army, Lieutenant Edward Vandenberg. I'm just taking a drive while I wait for my flight back home."

Two-Chins looked over at the soapy Toyota. "Why were you talking to the boy? Where is the boy?"

"He went inside. I think you scared him. I was just offering him five hundred dollars cash for his truck."

They glanced at each other. It was an eloquent glance. Whiskers said, "Five hundred dollars cash?"

"For his Toyota truck." They were confused now. They were trying to fit it together but all they could think about was the five hundred bucks, which was probably more than they made in a year. "I have it here," I pulled out my wallet again, and repeated, "in cash."

They came closer, frowning at my wallet. Their hands were still on their weapons, but they hadn't drawn them yet.

"You see," I said, "I need a truck."

I was about to pull out the cash and offer it to them for their Jeep. Not the best plan but the best I could come up with in that moment. But Two-Chins pulled his Glock, aimed it at me and scowled.

"Emanuel, take his wallet! He was trying to bribe us! You saw that!"

Emmanuel, with his whiskers and his moustache, inched forward, snatched the wallet from my hands and handed it over to Two-Chins, who peered inside and grinned.

"He got about two thousand dollars in here, credit card, driving license from America."

Emmanuel pulled his own weapon. They both looked real hyped. I smiled. "What you need now is a good excuse to shoot me, so you can hang on to that stuff and sell my passport and my driving license to your Iranian clients. Am I right?"

"I don't need an excuse to shoot you, American dog. You resisted ar—"

I snapped, "Holster your weapons, *now!*"

I knew they wouldn't do it, but men in uniform are conditioned to obey orders, and when they hear one issued with authority, they automatically respond. So I knew I had one, maybe two seconds of paralysis to work with. It was enough. The long step, slightly to the right of his weapon while my left hand grabbed the barrel and levered down, half a second. Slight twist on the ball of my right foot, and the right hook that almost took off Two-Chins' head, another half second. Slight adjustment of the angle of the Glock and pull the trigger, twice. One and a half seconds total.

Emmanuel sagged to the ground, bleeding profusely from his chest. Two-Chins was on the road, groaning. I angled my foot and stamped hard on the back of his neck. I took their weapons and fished the key from Two-Chins' pocket, then I climbed in behind the wheel of the jeep. On the back seat I saw a plastic groceries bag with a couple of sandwiches in it. I thought about the cell phone buried in the jungle and sat a moment thinking ahead and eating the sandwiches.

Finally I wrapped the cell I had kept in the grocery bag and, two minutes later, I was hurtling down the main highway, back toward the fringes of the Congo rain forest, wondering what the hell I was going to do, how the hell I was going to do it, and when I'd done it, what the hell I was going to do next. One thing that is drummed into every special ops guy from day one is, if you have not got an extraction plan, you are on a suicide mission.

I had been making it up as I went along from the moment they told me Claire had been taken. From the moment they killed the British troops who were escorting us, and took me prisoner, I had barely even been doing that. Now I was hurtling back to the camp with a crazy idea of how I was going to grab her, but what then? How the hell was I going to get her out?

One thing had been clear from the start. The Burunda regime was playing ball with Otropoco as well as with Russia and Iran, and the British governor—if he was still in the country—was of little concern. I had no idea how the British government had responded to the disappearance of fifty of their men in the Congo jungle, but I didn't imagine they'd be real happy about it.

Mind you, I reminded myself, the days of the Iron Lady were

long gone. The little I knew of the current crew in Westminster, they'd be apologizing to President George Majok for any offence they might have caused by being there in the first place. Either way, I could not count on help or support from the Brits or the Americans. This was something I had to do on my own.

How?

By the time I had pulled off the road and concealed the Jeep in among the trees half a mile from the camp, I still hadn't found an answer. I slung the bag with the C4 and the Glocks I'd taken from the cops in it over my shoulder, and started making my slow, laborious way through the dense undergrowth. It was heavy going, muggy and hot, and there was no path to follow. It was a case of picking my way over twigs, branches and fallen trees as silently as I could, pushing aside leaves the size of small aircraft carriers, or squeezing past branches with four-inch-long thorns which might or might not have been poisonous. And all the while trying to make sure any noise I made was irregular and arrhythmic.

The compass on my watch kept me going in roughly the right direction, otherwise I might have spent the rest of my life out there, going round in circles. But eventually I came to a fast-flowing stream which I knew was the camp's source of water. In many places you could only hear it, because it was overgrown with creepers and twisted tree trunks. In other places you could scramble down the bank to the river itself. It was maybe nine or ten feet across and waist deep.

Its depth and the speed at which it was flowing suggested it might join a larger river nearby. I filed the possibility away and retraced my steps to a large tree that leaned across the river and allowed me to cross without getting wet. I managed to scramble over OK and then dropped about six feet to the ground. That made a noise but I lay motionless for five minutes and nothing happened, so I moved on.

Jungles are not quite places. There are noises going on all the time, but about the only animal that makes a rhythmic, regular noise is the human being. And that is what you have to listen for.

Because we are also the most dangerous animal you are likely to find in the jungle.

It was a few minutes after I had crossed the river that I first caught sight of the narrow footpath. Visibility was poor because of the density of the undergrowth, but the path was visible some thirty feet away because the area had been cleared to get access to the water. That was when I heard the regular, slow rhythmic trudge of boots. I sprinted twenty feet and slipped in among the ferns and the foliage. I let go the bag, pulled my bowie knife and listened.

Two sets of boots. Two men, probably soldiers, coming for water. It was late afternoon, dark in a couple of hours. They were probably stocking up for the night.

They entered the forest about six feet from me. They were big, in camouflage pants and shirts, and big black boots. Each carried an assault rifle, a sidearm and a knife. And each of them carried two collapsible, three-or-four-gallon water containers with spigots.

One of the guys waited up top while the other slid down to the water and started filling the containers. I waited too. They didn't talk much, and what they did say I didn't understand. But after about ten minutes the tone of what they said, and the way they moved, said they were done filling, and now they were laden down with about a hundred and sixty pounds of water between them.

I slipped out before the nearest guy turned around. I didn't go for anything fancy. It had to be quick and it had to be silent. So I rammed the big, broad blade of the bowie knife right through the vertebrae in the back of his neck. Whatever his brain told him he ought to be doing in those final seconds, the message never got through.

As I wrenched the blade out, a quarter of a second later, I kicked him hard in his back and he toppled down on his pal below. I went down after him. His pal had dropped the water and was backing away, saying, "Eh! Eh!" Maybe two seconds had passed. He gaped at me as I came over the top of his collapsed friend and I kicked him hard in the head. He fell back in the river and as I landed next to him I drove the blade deep into his chest and twisted it right and left.

I grabbed the assault rifles and the sidearms, and was about to heave the bodies downstream when I had a thought. I searched in their pockets and after a moment I found what I was looking for. I took it, gave the bodies a heave, and scrambled out of the water to collect my bag, withdrew twenty feet back the way I had come and started crawling on my belly, through the ferns and trees, toward where I now knew the camp was.

It was after some ten minutes of painfully slow progress that I finally saw the camp. Thirty yards of grass, about two or three foot high, separated me from the huts. It wasn't hard to identify Otropoco's hut, and taking that as a reference I calculated where Claire's hut was. Then I started to crawl.

I crawled slowly, because rapidly moving grass is even more of a giveaway than rhythmic noise, and it took me all of two minutes to reach the back of Otropoco's hut. There I packed four pounds of C4 against the wall, stabbed in the remote detonator and grabbed a couple of heavy rocks from nearby to improvise a directional charge.

Then I moved along the backs of the huts till I was near the point where the path left the camp for the river. Here I used two of the remaining four pounds to make balls about an inch in diameter which I attached to fuse cord in three long strings, each with a detonator. Two I tossed onto the roofs of two of the huts and the third I left in the grass.

It was going to be quite a show. "Go out with a bang, Harry," I told myself. "Go out with a big bang."

I lay flat on my belly, pulled my phone from my pocket, scrolled to the keypad and pressed 9.

EIGHTEEN

FOUR POUNDS OF C4 WILL BLOW THE FRONT OF A bricks and mortar house. This pack smacked the air and ripped the walls and the roof of Otropoco's shack. In the movies explosions take several seconds to unfold in great, rumbling fireballs. In reality it's not like that. It takes maybe half a second, it cracks the air and, if doesn't kill you, it leaves you feeling dazed and badly shaken.

I staggered to my feet as the smoke cleared and scrambled around the corner into the main square of the camp. It was thick with smoke and dust kicked up by the detonation, but there was nobody about. They were still stunned and recovering from the shock. I ran straight for Claire's hut. As I drew close I could just make out two shadowy figures lying in the dirt. One was stretched out and motionless. The other was in the fetal position, rocking and moaning. I knelt beside him and confirmed he was one of the guard. Then I drove my knife into the side of his neck, severing the artery and the jugular.

I checked the other guy and saw he had a bad head injury but he was still alive. I cut his throat too and stood. I knew there was a padlock on Claire's door. I found it and as I lined it up with the Sig I heard voices across the square. Some were shouting, others were moaning and crying. I paused and pulled out my phone. I hit 8 on my keypad. That set off one of the strings of eight one-ounce balls of C4 I had left on the roof. It sounded like very powerful automatic fire outside the compound, on the far side, and I hoped it would draw their attention long enough for me and Claire to get away. From the shouts and screams I thought maybe it had worked.

I shot the lock, inched the door open and called softly, "Claire? It's me, Harry. Are you OK?" There was total silence. "Claire?"

A wave of sick nausea washed over me at the thought that she might have been in Otropoco's hut. But then a small voice said, "Harry?"

I moved in fast. "Yes, where are you?"

"*Harry!*" She rushed at me and clung to me. I was hearing more voices outside. Now they were running, shouting instructions. I pressed 7 while she clung to me, and set off another row of fireworks.

"Honey," I rasped, "we have no time. You have to get a grip and run like hell. Come on."

I pulled open the door. The smoke and dust were clearing and I could see men streaming past, making for the track to the river. I grabbed her wrist and scrambled out of the door, pulling her after me, and headed for the back of the hut. There we ran headlong toward the other entrance to the compound, the main entrance where we had entered in the Land Rovers before. When we got there I stopped, snapped at Claire, "Lie down!" and peered around the side of the first hut. The dust was practically gone and I could see almost all the men down at the far end. Some were trying to pick their way into the rubble that was all that was left of Otropoco's hut, while most of them were hanging around the exit toward the river.

I thought about opening fire on them, but instead I pulled the disposable lighter I had taken from the dead soldier at the river, and set fire to the thatch of the hut. It took a moment to catch, but once the breeze caught it the flames surged and thick smoke began to billow.

For a fraction of a second I weighed up the conflicting advantages of silence and secrecy, and taking out the tires of a couple of their vehicles. Secrecy won and I whispered, "Come on! Let's go!"

I grabbed her wrist again and we sprinted away from the village. Behind us I could hear more screaming and shouting. After fifteen or twenty yards I lurched left across the track and we plunged in among the thick undergrowth, headed roughly in the direction where I had left the Jeep. I was aware Claire had barely said a word since I'd broken into her hut. She was probably going into shock, and I knew I needed to keep her with me. I spoke as we went.

"OK, baby. You need to focus hard on what I am telling you. OK?"

She didn't say anything.

"Make the effort to answer me, Claire. Answer quietly, but I need you to keep responding, OK?"

"OK."

We were picking our way painfully slowly over uneven ground and foliage so dense you could barely see six feet ahead of you.

"Their village is on fire, and I think Otropoco is dead, so they are going to be focused hard on putting out the fire. The only water they have is a river thirty or forty yards from the camp. So they are going to be delayed, and that will give us a chance to make some headway. You understand?"

"Yes."

"Now what we need to do is try to be as quiet as possible, but move as fast as possible. You with me?"

"Yes, OK."

"That's good. You're doing fine."

"Stop talking. I'll let you know if shock starts kicking in."

I glanced back to give her a smile, but she didn't see. We pressed on.

By the time we had circled around and come to the stream, we could hear the sounds of heavy diesel engines moving on the road. There were not many of them, I only counted two, but any hope they'd give up on the search for us was obviously a forlorn one.

We found an opening in the vines, ferns and thick leaves and slid down the bank to wade across the water, which here was almost chest deep. At the far side we staggered out and scrambled up the muddy slope. The light was fading fast and I took a moment to orientate myself, then headed off again, with the sound of the trucks growing louder. That told me we were going in roughly the right direction.

After five minutes I finally spotted the Jeep through the giant leaves and the tree trunks. I hissed to Claire, "*Lie down on your belly. If anything happens, run!*"

I pulled my knife and, sliding on my belly I slipped through the undergrowth until I was practically under the truck. Then I pulled myself up, trying to keep in the wing mirror's blind spot, and pulled open the driver's door. There was no one in there, in the passenger's seat or in the back. I called softly to Claire, "OK, let's go."

She got up and moved to me, and I opened the rear door.

"I want you to get in, lie on the floor and wait for me. There is something I have to do."

"What?" she said. "Do what?"

I handed her one of the Glocks. "It is loaded and cocked. All you have to do is—"

"Harry, I'm from Wyoming. I know how to shoot a gun. What do you have to do?"

"When we left, as the roofs were catching light, I thought I saw two guys pulling Otropoco from the rubble."

"Harry, no."

"If he were dead, either they'd all be trying to put out the fire, or they'd all be hightailing it out of here. That's not happening. They are putting out the fire *and* looking for us. That means he's still alive."

"Harry, please."

"He won't stop, Claire. He'll hunt for us both and he won't stop until he finds us."

"Can't we just—"

"There's more." She stared at me. I said, "There is a nuclear device he wanted me to take to DC. I buried it not far from here. Otropoco has the detonator. If he is alive..."

"Oh, sweet God..."

"Get in, lie down, give me half an hour. If I am not back by then, drive like crazy. Make for South Sudan and try to contact the British or the American troops there." I kissed her, pulled off my jacket and handed it to her. "My wallet is in there with two thousand bucks. I'll be back." I grinned. "Like the Terminator."

She climbed in the back and lay on the floor. I closed the door and moved off toward the road, where I had heard the two trucks. On the way I grabbed some mud from the river and smothered my face, my hair and my shirt with it. They were looking for me in a jacket with Claire. My hope was that an unrecognizable guy covered in mud might make them pause before shooting, because it could be one of their own. In situations like these seconds can mean the difference between life and death.

I came to the rutted, pitted mess that passed for a road here and stood listening. I could hear the rumble of an idling motor on my left and started running that way. In my waistband I had my Sig and over my shoulder I had an HK 416 I had taken from some dead guy along the way. I also had the bag with four pounds of C4 in it. I thought briefly of the colonel and her constant complaint that I was always blowing things up. I wondered what she would think if she could see me now.

I ignored the small voice that said she would probably never see me again. I rounded a bend and saw the two trucks side by side, fifteen or twenty yards away, blocking the road. There were four guys there in fatigues carrying assault rifles. They stared at me and raised their weapons. I waved, making like I was exhausted and out of breath, and started pointing back toward the camp as I ran, getting closer two yards every second.

"They found them!" I yelled. "Down the river."

The nearest guy, huge with a red beret, took a step closer, scowling. "Who found them? Who was searching the river?"

I was fifteen feet away, staggering, making like I was out of breath. "The fire!" I said, "It's spreading. They sent me to get you."

The light was failing and he was staring hard at my face. He drew breath, but nobody ever heard what he was going to say because I shot him through the head. He was blocking me from the view of two of the other guys, but the fourth was over at the back of the second truck. He saw what I did and he reacted immediately by making an inarticulate noise and raising his rifle to his shoulder. By the time it got there his brains were erupting out of the back of his head. I had calculated the sequence of my shots long before I'd got there.

I dropped to my knees as the red beret keeled over and saw the other two guys both training their weapons on me. They were good. They had not wasted time getting over their surprise.

I flopped left behind the front wheel of the Land Rover as the rounds tore up the dirt. That gave me a clear view of two boots. I tore out one of the ankles with a single slug and as the last guy came around the hood of the truck I plugged him four times in the chest.

I was up before he hit the ground , and went to look for the guy with the shattered ankle. He was crying and moaning. I knelt on his hip and placed the muzzle of the Sig on his knee.

"I'm in a hurry," I said. "Answer right or I'll blow your leg in half."

"Help me. Is a lot of hurt."

"Is Otropoco alive?"

He nodded a lot. "He's hurt, hurt bad. Please help me."

I helped him by ending his pain. Then I grabbed the Land Rover and drove fast, over the rust and through the mud and puddles, skidding and swerving across the road, back toward the camp, as darkness closed in.

NINETEEN

THE CAMP, OR VILLAGE OR WHATEVER IT WAS, WAS ablaze. Thick smoke was billowing everywhere and long fingers and tongues of flame reached up toward the black sky. I roared into the middle of the town. There was nobody there. The smoke was too thick. But there were people crowded down by the path to the river, forming a human chain, hurling buckets of water onto the few huts that were not yet in flames. I skidded to a halt and jumped out. The roar and crackle of the flames was deafening and the heat was overpowering. Nobody took any notice of me. I grabbed the nearest guy and screamed at him over the noise of the conflagration, "*Where is the boss? Where is Otropoco?*"

"*By the river! Leave him now! He is dying! Bring water!*"

I nodded. "*I will!*"

I ran. I ran along the line of men heaving buckets and every kind of utensil they could muster to get water to the flames. And as I approached the opening, where I had killed the two first men, I saw him, crumpled by the roadside in the long grass. He looked grotesque and broken, and for a moment I thought maybe he was dead. I crouched by his side and raised his head. His eyes focused on me. He croaked a couple of times, then managed, "I knew you'd come."

"I can't let you live."

He made a grotesque chuckle and nodded. "And then there's the detonator."

"Where is it?"

"In the rubble, in all the mess in my room, that you made. Maybe you triggered it. Maybe because of you there is a radioactive cloud now over Morocco, or Spain."

The next steps were clear. Discreetly kill him and go to look for the detonator. I reached for my knife but he laughed his sick laugh again. "Or," he said, "is it in my pocket? Or did I give it to someone with instructions to detonate it in seven hours' time? What do you think, Harry?"

I made a cradle of my left leg, so my back was to the human chain and I obscured Otropoco's head and chest from view, not that I believed anybody was bothering to watch us. I pulled my knife from my boot and took in it my left hand, where it was supporting his head. There was a look almost of relief in his single eye as he watched me do it. I said:

"There is no way I can ever make you tell me where it is, is there?" He shook his head. "Not torture, nor begging, nor appealing to what shreds of humanity you might have left. You will never tell me."

"Never." He made a strange noise and I realized that he was weeping.

"Otropoco, I have no religion. But I heard once that the Buddhists believe that your last thought conditions what your next life is going to be." He was shaking now with his sobbing and had his face turned away. I placed the tip of the knife on his left collarbone and told him, "I want you to think that whatever horrors made you become what you have become, somewhere inside you was a spark of the divine flame, and in a different world you might have been a decent guy."

His weeping stopped and he stared at me with his one, horrific eye, and I slipped the blade in hard and fast, severing arteries and veins and skewering his heart.

I felt in his pockets and found the detonator where I had expected it to be. Right there in his jacket, to hand. I half ran back along the line to the town, swung in behind the wheel and took off the way I had come. As I sped through the smoke and the roaring flames something began to dawn on me. They had lost control of the fire. It was increasingly clear there was nothing they could do to stop it.

How long before they gave up? And how long before hopelessness and failure, and Otropoco's murdered body, turned their minds to revenge? I drove too fast. The Land Rover's headlamps swayed and swung across the potholes, the looming trees and the mud-strewn puddles the size of small lakes. I skidded, slid and jumped, hurtling back to where I had left the four dead soldiers.

And suddenly they were there, lying in the mud, with the other truck half on the track and half in the forest. I grabbed my bag and pulled out the four remaining pounds of C4. I selected a tripwire detonator, climbed out leaving the explosive under the back seat and looped the tripwire through all four doors before tying it to the driver's door. If any of them was opened, I'd hear about it, however far away I was.

Then I ran, scrambling through the jungle, not caring anymore if I made a noise. I found the jeep and hammered on the glass and on the door, half shouting, *"Let's go! Let's go! Let's go!"*

I wrenched open the back door and found her shivering badly. I pulled her out, grabbed my jacket and wrapped her in it and made her get in the passenger seat.

"Belt! You'll need it!"

Then I was behind the wheel, spinning the Jeep around and roaring for the road. We hit the road, lurched, bounced and skidded. Claire screamed but I ignored her and plowed through a puddle a foot deep. Water sprayed over the windshield, blinding me to what little of the road I could see. I hit the wipers and sprayed water and a filthy opening appeared, showing me blackness, dimly illuminated by the funnels of amber glow from the headlamps.

Pitch shadows showed black holes, rocks and furrows that loomed too fast to avoid them. I drove fast and every impact was jarring and painful, but what I most feared was damaging a wheel or an axel rod. If they caught us now, imagination was the only limit to what they would do to us.

The road dipped steeply. I cursed myself for not remembering the dip. A small stream ran along the bottom. We hit it at speed and for a few seconds the world disappeared. Claire stifled a scream. As we surged out the other side the wheels spun in the wet and the mud, and for a few seconds we started to slide back. I dropped gear, the wheels gripped and we started to climb. I hit the wipers to full and sprayed water on the windshield again.

A smudged, streaked gap in the mud showed the dark, tangled road ahead. The surface was bad, but not as bad as what we'd just left behind. Then the air shook: one detonation followed by another, and then another as a fireball rose into the sky behind us, lighting up the mirrors and the whole cab.

For a second I dared to hope. The C4 plus the two gas tanks, had that taken care of them? Would they give up now? I accelerated and kept glancing in the rearview mirror. Sickness twisted my gut. There was a glow among the trees. It wasn't the glow of the burning trucks. It was the glow of headlamps. Headlamps that were in pursuit. I swore violently in my head and fought to stay focused. What was next along the road? Where could I turn off and lose them?

The village.

A feeling of dread overwhelmed me. These bastards, in the crazed state of mind they were in, could not be allowed to enter the village. If they entered the village asking for us, there would not be a man, woman or child left alive by morning. And that meant one thing.

When they reached the village I had to be close enough for them to see. And I had to kill them. Every damned one of them.

A plan started to form in my head and suddenly I knew exactly what I had to do. The village appeared and slipped past in the dark. I could see their headlamps closing, maybe half a mile away. The road had improved but I slowed, allowing them to get closer, until I could make out the sets of headlamps. There were three of them, driving like they were crazy, swerving, jumping the potholes and rocks. I knew the state of mind they were in. I'd been there a few times myself. You don't care what happens to you. You don't care if you get maimed or die. Just so long as you can kill along the way.

We'd passed the village and I knew that up ahead there were a couple of turns on the right that would lead me to the approximate location where I had buried the bomb. I didn't know when they would arrive. But I knew that when they did, Claire had to be there for them to get her the hell out of Burunda.

The turn loomed out of the darkness among the reaching fingers of gnarled trees. A glance at the mirror told me they were less than a quarter of a mile behind me. I slammed on the brakes and spun the wheel, and fishtailed into the track. It was narrow and rutted and the trees pressed in from the sides.

Claire said, "Where are you going?"

I snapped, "Cover your eyes!"

I didn't need to tell her twice. She covered her face with her arms. I pulled the Sig and shot the windshield, then punched it out until it fell over the hood. After that I killed the lights and by that time I saw the three trucks pulling into the track behind me, maybe three hundred yards away.

Without the windshield I could see clearly and I hit the gas, pulling away from them now. I pulled the burner cell from my pocket, tried one-handed to pull it free from the grocery bag, and scrolled with my right thumb, looking for the marked location. It wasn't easy with the truck lurching and jumping on the uneven track.

I found it and tapped just as Claire screamed. I looked up and slammed on the brakes too late. We hit the bank, jumped a foot in the air and slid sideways down the muddy slope toward the black, swirling water.

The water surged in through the open windshield and in seconds the Jeep began to sink. The current wasn't powerful, but it was enough to drag us forward. I shoved the cell back in the bag and into my pocket, yelling at Claire, "*Get out! Get out!*" as I tried to scramble from behind the wheel. I saw her disappear through the opening and wrenched my pants free from the handbrake. The truck went down and I exploded up to the surface.

"*Claire!*"

"*Here!*"

I saw the rough form of her head bobbing a few feet from me and swam toward her. "*Give me your hand!*"

We grabbed at each other and I hissed in her ear. "They're right behind us. We have to make it to the far bank. In silence, honey! Don't make a sound."

We let the current take us slowly through the darkness, and as we went we pulled silently for the far side. It was maybe a hundred feet away, but the pull of the water and the need for silence made it hard work. As we went I saw the glow of the approaching head-lamps and heard the whine of diesel. Seconds later there was the screech of brakes, and the slamming of doors tore the night like gunfire.

Then there were flashlights. First they played on the muddy bank, and when they found the skid marks there were shouts and screams. Then the probing beams of the flashlights began to play on the water, searching for the truck and growing ever closer.

Then one of the beams picked up the rear wing of the Jeep. There were more shouts and shrieks. Some asshole let fly a burst of automatic fire, and another asshole followed suit. I prayed to some nameless god that they would be satisfied with the crashed Jeep, and for a moment it seemed they might be. But it just took one of them to start searching wider with his flashlight, for the others to do the same.

I knew then that I was going to have to kill them. I counted them. There were ten of them, and three flashlights. The beams of which, among shouted comments and pointing hands, were moving downstream and across the river toward us.

"*When I say,*" I whispered to Claire, "*go under and swim for the far bank.*" We stared at each other for a moment. I added, "*Stay under as long as you can, high velocity rounds disintegrate when they hit the water. But Claire?*"

"*What?*"

"*Don't make a noise when you surface.*" The terror was patent on her face. I pulled the cell from my pocket and gave it to her. "*I don't know if it will work, baby. Try to dry it and find the marked location. Failing that, call Buddy. Just in case I don't make it.*"

I slipped it in the back pocket of her jeans and we kept moving, swimming slowly and silently toward the far shore. And all the while I watched the circles of light playing on the water, moving ever closer. It was clear in my mind that just before they found us I had to send Claire across, and I had to go back and take them out. I knew there was a chance the phone was not going to work, but if she managed to dry it out she might just be able to call the brigadier.

On the other hand, the chances of my taking out ten well-armed mercenaries with nothing but a semi-automatic and a bowie knife were practically nil. The important point, though, the one that was weighing on my mind, was that they were after me, not Claire. And once they had me they might just let her go.

Then three things happened all at once. One of the circles of light darted toward us, I hissed, "*Now!*"

And across the water, on the far side where she needed to go, I heard the unmistakable slosh of crocodiles slipping into the water.

TWENTY

THERE HAVE BEEN MOMENTS IN MY LIFE WHEN I HAVE done things I did not believe I was capable of doing. When the imperative urge to survive kicks in, we can dig deep and find resources we didn't know we had. When the life we are trying to save is not our own, but that of a person we care for, we are able to dig deeper still.

But in that moment, stuck in a deep, black river, with armed men showering us with automatic fire, and crocodiles swimming out to meet us, I did truly believe I had reached the end of the road.

I plunged deep, pulling Claire down with me. High-velocity rounds to not penetrate deep into water. But we felt them and saw them erupt above us. We were going to die. I knew that. But I also knew that if there was a fighting chance for Claire to reach the bank I had to try. So I pushed her on and kicked to the surface, pulling the Sig as I went. As I broke out of the water I took aim.

A lot of people believe you can't fire a semi-automatic that has been submerged. It's a fallacy. Since the invention of cartridge ammunition, you can get your weapon wet and then fire it. And that was what I did. I let off six rounds in the general direction of the nearest guy's chest. Four of them caught him and he fell into the water.

Crocodiles have a very highly developed sense of smell and can smell blood from a considerable distance. So right then, the guy I had shot was their primary focus of attention. As the nine remaining guys screamed and scrambled down the muddy slope to reach their pal, I found Claire, took a hold of her and started swimming toward the far bank, making as little movement as I could. And as our feet found the mud at the river's edge, thirty or forty feet away the thrashing started as the huge beast tore the body apart.

Then the engines revved and the trucks reversed away.

We clambered up away from the water, slipping and falling, clinging to roots and vines to pull ourselves up. Until we fell into the darkness of the jungle. There we clung to each other for what felt like a blessed eternity, but was probably no more than ten or fifteen seconds.

Then I kissed her and whispered, "Come on, we have to keep moving."

We walked for maybe ten or fifteen minutes making painfully slow progress through the dark. My purpose right then was to get as far as possible from our pursuers, in the hope that they would eventually give up on us. Once or twice we stopped and thought we heard the sound of the trucks, but it was hard to be sure, and impossible to know from what direction the sounds came.

Eventually we came to a hollow that was partly covered by fallen trees and vines. Claire was shivering badly from shock and I told her to sit. I gathered what twigs and branches I could and, using the disposable lighter I had used to burn the camp, I lit a small fire. We sat close and I asked her for the phone.

When I pulled it from the plastic bag it was damp, but not as wet as I had feared. And after fifteen minutes close to the flames its mild psychosis seemed to pass. I found the location I had set and glanced at Claire.

"We're only about two miles from where we need to be. How are you doing?"

She glanced at me, then nodded. "I'll be OK."

I called the brigadier.

"Harry. Where are you?"

"I'm in the jungle with Claire. We're two miles from the location. I have the detonator and Otropoco is dead."

"Excellent work, as always."

"But we have nine men hunting for us in trucks. I hope we've lost them, but I can't be sure."

"How's your battery?"

"Low."

"Don't waste it. We have a team on the way to extract the bomb. I'm sure they'd like to have the detonator too. You'd better get moving."

"OK." I hung up. I watched Claire a moment. She was still shaking badly. Two miles in normal conditions would take forty minutes, fifty if you were strolling. But through dense rain forest at night, while suffering from shock, it was going to be a major effort.

"If we're going to get out of here we need to get moving."

She nodded but she didn't move. I stood and kicked out the fire, then helped her to her feet.

We walked for half an hour, and then the unexpected happened. We came to a track that led in the same direction my cell was telling me to go. The track wasn't huge, barely wide enough for a truck, and it didn't look like it was frequently used, but as I hunkered down to look by the light of my cell, there was at least one set of tire tracks that was fresh. It was an insane decision, but it was the only decision open to me. I looked up at Claire and thought that before long I was going to have to carry her.

"This track seems to lead where we're going, or at least close, but it looks like it has been used very recently. If we follow it, we can get there in maybe half an hour or twenty minutes. But,

Claire, if we hear anything, I need you to respond. You need to get under cover immediately and silently. Are you going to be able to do that?"

She nodded. "I'll do my best."

I helped her to her feet again and we set off at a brisk walk. The track was comparatively straight and at times the undergrowth closed in, giving us a strange, and completely unfounded, sense of security.

We didn't talk, and all the way I kept Claire at my side or in front of me, gently propelling her when she began to slow. She didn't complain, and though I knew her state of shock had drained her completely, she never asked to stop.

After another twenty or thirty minutes the path began to veer to the right, but the needle on my cell told me we needed to go left, and that our objective was no more than seventy or eighty feet away.

We came off the road and started picking our way through comparatively thin undergrowth. It seemed this had been a track once, but now it was overgrown with saplings and ferns, and hanging vines. After a minute or less we came to a clearing. I stopped, checked my cell.

"We're here."

I guided Claire to a large tree, settled her and went to look for the spot where I had buried the device. It was there, undisturbed, and I had a sick feeling in my belly knowing that in my pocket was the detonator that could explode that device and level everything in an area of over two miles, and spread radioactive death many miles beyond that.

I returned and sat by Claire's side. She was still shivering. I laid her against me, put my arms around her and called the brigadier again.

"Harry."

"We're here. What's the ETA?"

"Imminent. They are over the Border and into Burunda."

"OK, I'll let you know when they get here."

I hung up, and just seconds later started hearing the hum of motors. But it was not choppers. As I listened to the growing hum I knew it was diesel engines, driving through the forest. And among the chaos of thoughts that tumbled through my mind in that moment, one that leapt to the fore was, how? How did they know where to come? And, how did they come so close and not find it?

I grabbed Claire and dragged her up. "On your feet, Doc! Give me the Glock." She handed it over as I shoved her to the ground. "Get under the bushes. Stay there and don't make a sound! The cavalry are on their way!"

I shoved her in among some ferns and hanging ivy. When she was sufficiently out of sight I jumped, grabbed a branch and hauled myself up just as the glow of headlamps swelled through the branches.

TWENTY-ONE

THEY PLOWED THROUGH THE UNDERGROWTH, TEARING down vines and saplings, and erupted into the clearing. The first of the trucks, a Land Rover turned to the right, the second looked like a Nissan and turned left. The third was a pickup, either a Hilux or a Ford Ranger stopped in the middle, a little to my right.

I didn't pause to think. There was no time for thinking. I jumped. It wasn't a huge jump: seven feet to my right and a drop of no more than five or six feet. I landed with my legs akimbo and the Glock held in both hands, and double-tapped through the roof, two on the driver's side and two into the passenger, and then again, two into the driver and two into the passenger.

I didn't wait to see the result. I dropped and rolled and let myself fall off the back of the truck. Within seconds I could hear slamming doors and shouting. It must have been pretty confusing. The way they had positioned the trucks they were illuminating the whole clearing. But they had also placed the trucks behind glaring headlamps and spots. The shots had apparently come from nowhere. No windshields had smashed, and so far no victims had appeared.

So far.

Acting fast I blew off the gas tank cap, took my knife and

ripped off a piece of sleeve which I stuffed into the hole, then slipped under the pickup, telling myself there were still seven bad guys left. Across the clearing they had climbed out, four from the Nissan and three from the Land Rover. They were shouting a lot and I figured they were waving their assault rifles too, but all I could see was three pairs of feet. Which meant there were four pairs of feet I couldn't see, but two got you twenty they were standing around their truck, shouting and waving their AK-47s.

I took aim and put two rounds through one shin. The scream was horrific and the guy fell to the ground with his leg twisted at a grotesque angle. By that time I had put another two rounds through another shin and that guy was also down and screaming.

Five.

I could have stayed there and tried for a couple of head shots on the guys who were down. But they were out of action and I was badly outnumbered. I had to keep moving. And moving meant in a way they did not expect.

I scrambled back, got to my feet and hunkered down, set light to my length of sleeve stuck in the gas tank. Then I ran for the back of the Nissan.

I was still in the shadows to them, and they were still in the full glare of their own headlamps; and when the huge flames suddenly *whoomphed* at the back of the pickup, all their attention was focused there. I could have take out a couple of them right there and then, but I knew my luck was running out and I was sailing real close to the wind.

I dropped and rolled and came up on one knee, facing back toward the Toyota. It was starting to burn big time. The gas was hot and there were lots of fumes. I knew and they knew it was going to blow at any second. I could see them all now. The one guy left from the Land Rover, and the four guys from the Nissan, all protecting their faces with their arms and backing away from the surging flames.

I shot the one at the back. His head whiplashed and his brains sprayed into the firelight. They all looked around at each other.

The roar of the fire was becoming furious. Now there was confusion. I shot the one nearest to me through the back of his skull. His face sprayed over the guy standing next to him.

Three.

I was hissing under my breath, "*Now! Now! Now!*"

That was when they saw me and charged, firing as they ran. The Toyota was supposed to explode and it had let me down. Now I was in big trouble. I sprang to the far side of the Nissan and fell to the ground. There were ten legs running maybe ten or fifteen feet away and I fired indiscriminately at all of them. There was a scream. Somebody fell.

And that was when the Toyota exploded, showering burning fuel high into the air. A second later there was more screaming and in the glaring, dancing light I saw the diabolical image of one of the remaining two men staggering horrifically, engulfed in flames. I took aim, to put him out of his agony, but he dropped to the ground and lay still.

A rustle behind me and I turned. The last guy, with a mass of dreadlocks and wild crazy eyes. I didn't hesitate. The action was automatic. I raised the gun and pulled the trigger.

It went click, click.

He grinned and that was when I noticed he had a machete hanging from his belt. He slung the assault rifle over his shoulder, took the machete, and with an expression of pure hatred and frenzy on his face, he rushed me, screaming.

I hurled the Glock at him and he batted it away. Then he was on me, slashing diagonally right and left. I backed up in two strides, but charging forward he was always going to be faster than me running backward. Not only that, holding the machete his reach was about four foot.

Running was not an option. Staying put was not an option. So I charged.

The fact is, swinging a sword or a machete at the same time as running is not easy. You either have to swing or run, not both. So Dreadlocks had gone for the bayonet charge, and as he did that I sprang forward and slightly to my right, into his guard. I delivered a right hook to his head that would have put a rhinoceros to sleep. But this guy rolled with it, did some fancy footwork and brought the damned machete crashing down toward my neck.

I managed to grab his wrist with my left hand, but the iron blade cut into my shoulder. The pain was excruciating and the injury would have been a lot worse if I hadn't kicked him hard in the belly at the same time. He fell back. I yelled with the pain and went after him. He rushed forward, plunging the tip toward my belly. I sidestepped, but the razor-sharp blade sliced into my abdomen as it passed. The agony morphed into rage and I smashed my left fist into his windpipe. He staggered back, wheezing and I went after him, not thinking, just driven by pain and fury.

I grabbed his wrist again and pounded my right fist into his face twice. Then I turned his wrist against the joints so he bent forward with his elbow locked, and bellowed as I smashed my forearm down on the joint. He screamed through his semi-paralyzed throat and partly released his grip on the machete. I grabbed the hilt and twisted it out of his hand. I may have broken a couple of his fingers. I didn't care. I kicked him hard in the belly again and, as he went down on his knees, I roared, swung the blade and cut off his head.

I roared again as I watched it drop and roll. And by degrees I became aware that the whole clearing was bathed in brilliant light. I watched the kneeling, headless body keel over and drop. Then there was a huge noise and a furious gale and all the trees began to toss and sway. A disembodied voice yelled at me.

"Drop the weapon and get down on your knees!"

I threw down the machete and raised my open hands. Ropes suddenly coiled down out of the glaring light and men in camouflage with helmets and HK 416s dropped to the ground. One of them approached me with his weapon aimed at my chest. He shouted:

"Get down on your knees with your hands behind your head!"

I kept my hands raised but yelled back at him, *"You get on your goddamned knees! I am Sergeant Harry Bauer, of the British SAS! You're here because I called you!"*

"Get on your knees!"

"No!"

His captain approached at a run and told him to go help secure the area. The chopper rose and backed away some, reducing the downdraft. The noise was still like thunder, though. The captain spoke to me, shouting above the thud of the rotors.

"You're Bauer?"

"Yes."

"Captain Mitch Vaughn. Where's the device?"

I raised my index finger to him. *"First!"* I led him over to where I had left Claire and helped her out from under the bushes. She was trembling and crying and clung to me, repeating over and over, *"Oh God, Harry, you're alive. You're alive."*

I held her and turned to Vaughn. *"She goes back to the States. Brigadier Bird has cleared it with your brass."*

"This is Dr. Erickson?"

I nodded and we made our way back toward where the chopper was hovering. A couple of soldiers closed in and Claire was fitted with a harness. She was watching me, dazed, with terror in her eyes, clinging to me with her hands.

I held her tight and kissed her. "These guys are going to look after you, baby. In a few hours you'll be home. The brigadier will take care of everything."

Her voice was high, bordering on hysterical. *"But you're coming! Harry! You're coming too! You're coming with me!"*

"Yes! Yes!" I was nodding. *"There is just one thing I have to do first, and I will see you at the ranch in a couple of days."*

A voice said, *"Come on, guys!"* The winch whined and suddenly Claire was rising toward the chopper, screaming my name and reaching down for me. I hollered back, *"Two days! I'll see you at the ranch!"*

Vaughn placed his hand on my shoulder. "I'm sorry, Bauer, we haven't time for this."

I felt a flash of anger, but I knew he was right. I led him to the spot where I had buried the device. Two soldiers followed with spades. I pointed.

"*It's in there. Stainless steel cylinder so big.*" I showed them with my hands and they began to dig. I reached in my pocket and pulled out the detonator. "*This is the detonator. You need to put it in a box or something. And you need to isolate the bomb in a container where it cannot receive electronic signals.*"

He gave me the thumbs up and shouted, "*Ten four!*"

I watched them insert the device into a lines box, seal it and hoist it onto the chopper. The detonator was also secured and the men began to rise up on their cords, back into the chopper.

The captain placed his hand on my shoulder again.

"You sure you're not coming?"

I shook my head. "There still something to do. I have to end this."

He pointed to my arm and my belly. "You need medical attention."

"I'll see to it."

He looked around, at the flames and the carnage. "You did all this? On your own."

I nodded. "You should see the rest of it. This is just the tail end."

"You're serious." It wasn't a question.

I nodded, feeling suddenly weary. "Yeah. Take care of my girl, Captain."

"I will."

He rose up, with the rest of them, into the dark, unmarked helicopter and within a moment they were gone.

I walked back to Dreadlocks' beheaded body and took his assault rifle and his sidearm. I went first to the guy with the shattered shin who was lying by the smoldering Toyota. I felt his pulse, but he was dead. So I walked over to the first two I'd shot by the Land Rover. They were both still alive, though one of them was delirious and slipping into a coma. I spoke to his friend.

"Hey, look at me."

He turned to face me. He was weeping. I pointed all around me. "You see all this? I did it. This and your camp, and Otropoco and Van Hurt. I destroyed it all and I killed them all. See your friend?"

He looked at him and as he did so I shot the delirious guy in the head. His suffering stopped, and I hunkered down beside the last living member of the gang.

"You cannot save your lower leg, but if the doctors get to you soon, maybe they can just amputate at the knee. You will live, at least. You understand?"

He nodded, sobbing.

"So I need you to answer me a question."

"Anything. Ask. I tell."

"How did you know we were coming here?"

He half laughed, half wept, like he thought it was going to be a hard question, and it was so easy.

"The radar," he said. "The radar was tracking the helicopter and informed the office."

"The office—"

"Yeah, the office, the—"

I nodded. "I know what office."

I shot him in the head and made for the Land Rover. He wasn't going to be torturing anybody else, with one leg, two legs or one and a half legs. His game was over.

TWENTY-TWO

As I pulled out of the clearing, and started the jolting path toward the road to Apodo-Djamu, a roll of thunder tore the sky apart and a soft patter of rain soon became a steady downpour. The road was practically invisible, lost somewhere between the huge puddles that soon developed into a series of muddy streams, the rocks and ruts, and the sheets of rain that reflected my headlamps, reducing visibility to ten or fifteen feet. Despite that, at least until I hit the main highway, that invisible road was impossible to miss. Because it was the only place where there were no trees. I had the weird, frustrating feeling of grinding, struggling forward, without ever moving in the enveloping blackness.

And then, quite suddenly, the trees fell away and I was pulling onto the highway. The visibility was not much better, and without the dense forest either side it was sometimes hard to know exactly where the road was. But I had a driving sense that time was short and I floored the pedal, hurtling through the driving rain. It was crazy and reckless, but life doesn't always give you a choice. Anyone who tells you, *you always have a choice*, has never had a parachute that failed to open.

Somehow I made it alive, and as I approached the city streetlamps began to appear, like very tall, very thin luminous ghosts shrouded in silver needles of rain. I slowed as I moved through the filthy shantytowns, now several inches deep in mud. People, thin and incurious, perched on pallets and other bits of trash to keep them out of the water, sat under plastic or corrugated asbestos and watched me dive past.

The squalor gave way to the suburbs, where the palm trees and the banana trees tossed and swayed under the onslaught of the rain. There was not a person to be seen, only high walls and steel gates.

And then the immense towers of steel and glass rose up through the mist of the downpour. The streets were empty. There were barely even cars. It was like a scene from an apocalypse movie. A pedestrian crossing switched from green to red, reflected on the wet asphalt. I jumped the light, came to the main, central circus and turned down Independence Avenue.

The tropical gardens slid by on my right, the trees bowed by the rain, making black silhouettes against the streetlamps. On my left the great towers slid by. Restaurants and shop windows passed, with dull glowing windows, amber, red, violet and green.

I found a space, pulled in and parked. I climbed out of the Land Rover and in seconds I was drenched. The cut on my belly was a flesh wound, but as I stood it hurt like hell, and the gash in my shoulder was aching, debilitating. I crossed the sidewalk, leaving my blood in the rain on the sidewalk, and moved to the entrance to the tower where Better Tomorrows had their office. I expected it to be closed and was wondering about blowing out the lock, but I was lucky. The doors were still open though the porter had gone.

I returned to the truck and pulled out the assault rifle I'd taken from Dreadlocks.

I crossed the lobby and stepped into one of the elevators. The office was on the 16th floor. When the elevator finally came to a stop and I stepped out I had left an ugly pool of water and blood on the floor.

It was a broad landing with three big glass doors. The biggest was the one ahead of me. Better Tomorrows had not just glass doors, but glass walls too, and the walls were plastered with posters and photographs of happy, smiling kids standing outside brand-new schools and surrounded by fresh-faced smiling aid workers. Hopes, dreams, fantasies.

I pushed the door and, as I had expected, it was open. The reception was empty. The main lights were off, but there was enough light to see. On my right there was a corridor, and at the end of the corridor there was a door on the left that was open. Bright light streamed out and I could hear the murmur of voices.

I walked down the corridor and in through the open door. Again, as I had expected, Luis Camacho and Jean Fenlon were there. It was a large office with four desks, and the big, plate-glass doors were open onto a large balcony where the rain was pattering. The atmosphere was sultry, and Luis and Jean were busy disconnecting hard drives and packing them in boxes with physical files.

Jean just stared at me, but Luis got to his feet. He tried to smile, but seeing the state I was in, soaked, bruised, with my torn shirt soaked with blood, he must have thought better of it. Instead he said, "What the hell... *Harry?*"

"What's the matter, Luis? Did you think I was dead?"

His mouth tried to make several sentences, but failed on each one. I pointed at the boxes on the desks where they were packing the contents of the office.

"What are you doing?"

Luis licked his lips. Jean said, "We're moving the operation. After what happened to Claire..."

"What happened to Claire, Jean?"

She laughed and frowned at the same time, like she was confused. "Well, you know better than anyone—" She gestured at me. "What on Earth happened to you? You need a doctor."

I smiled, and by the expressions on their faces it was not a nice smile. "What happened to me? I'll tell you. I met Otropoco."

I waited, watching their faces. Absolutely nothing happened to their faces. They were rigid, like granite.

"He made a mistake," I said. "Him, and your pal Van Hurt. They both made mistakes. They kidnapped Claire and threatened to rape and torture her. Now, you see, the thing is, rape and torture are things that upset me."

She made a real effort. She tried hard to sound like she wasn't scared. "Did you find her? Is she OK...?"

"I killed the president of Tubdhaawi, but of course you know that."

They both shook their heads and licked their lips. Luis said:

"Harry, you're not making a lot of sense. Why don't you put the rifle down?"

I regarded him a moment, still smiling. "I'm not making sense? You make it sound like I'm crazy. Do you think I am psychotic, Luis? Psychotics can't tell the difference between reality and fantasy."

"Just take it easy, Harry."

"Was it a fantasy when Otropoco and Van Hurt handed over the tactical nuclear device?" They glanced at each other. If the device had been handed over, what the hell was I doing in Burunda instead of being vaporized aboard the plane? I went on. "Was it a fantasy when Van Hurt tried to find out who I worked for, and I choked him to death and broke his neck?" Now they went very still. You could see the sinking feeling on their faces. "When I buried the device in the jungle? Was it a fantasy when I blew Otropoco's hut with C4 and set fire to the camp? Was it fantasy when I stabbed Otropoco in the heart with my bowie knife? Was it, Luis, a fantasy when I took the detonator? *Was it fantasy,*" I allowed my voice to rise, "*when I killed the ten men who chased after us, when I put Claire aboard a US Navy chopper along with the device and the detonator? Was all that fantasy, Luis?*"

There was absolute silence in the room. I turned and looked at Jean.

"Was it fantasy when the last man I killed, pleading for his life, told me that they had known where to find us because you were informed by by the Burunda Air Force radar, and you informed them?"

I slung the rifle over my shoulder and pointed at Jean. "Sit down behind the desk. If you move I'll shoot you."

She sat. I turned to Luis. "I am going to tell you what fantasy is."

I stepped forward and backhanded him hard. He groaned and his eyes lost focus. I took a handful of his hair and dragged him out to the corridor. There I thrust his face at the glass and showed him the happy, smiling kids.

"That," I snarled, "is fantasy!" I am not proud of what I did, but my hands took on a life of their own and I smashed his face into the glass, shouting *"That is a fantasy!"* and then I couldn't stop. I must have done it five or six times, bellowing at him, *"And that! And that! And that is a fantasy!"*

I dragged him back into the office. He was groaning, trying to talk. I was still shouting at him. *"Can you fly, Luis? Is that a fantasy?"* I kicked the desk out of the way and sent Jean sprawling. *"I think you can fly! So why don't you fly back to your family in Mexico!"*

I grabbed the scruff of his neck and the seat of his pants and hurled him over. I guess sixteen stories was enough for him to work out the difference between reality and fantasy. When he hit the sidewalk in a grotesque, broken mess. I told him, "Give my regards to Otropoco and the cartel."

I went back into the office. Jean Fenlon had not run. Fear had paralyzed her. She was sitting on the floor staring at me with large, round eyes. I said, "Do I need to explain the difference between reality and fantasy to you?"

She gave her head a single shake. "No."

"Good. I'm old fashioned. I believe men should not hurt women. So I am going to give you a choice. You can call Colonel Fisher and have him come and finish boxing your stuff, and give yourself into custody to be tried for terrorism. Or I can send you after Luis. What's it going to be?"

She actually thought about it. I guess she figured she had enough to do some trading with the British and American authorities, because she said, "I'll talk to Fisher."

I pulled my damp cell from my pocket and called him myself. He answered on the second ring.

"Fisher."

"Colonel Fisher, this is Harry Bauer."

"Harry, what on Earth happened to you? And my men! We've been trying to—"

"Sir, I have a lot to tell you, but this is neither the time nor the place. You need to send some of your men over here. You need to be aware that you could have a situation on your hands and you need to tell the governor to arrange backup."

"Good lord! Are you serious?"

"I have here a ton of evidence and a live witness that will prove that Better Tomorrows was engaged in terrorism. I am going to put you in touch with Brigadier Bird who will confirm everything for you. Meantime I need you to send a team to the Better Tomorrows office to collect this material. It will implicate the government and the president, so you will need military backup. I also need to be to be in the States by tomorrow morning."

"I'll see what I can do. I'm on my way with a dozen men."

I hung up and called the brigadier.

"Report."

I filled him in and he said he'd call the colonel and make arrangements.

"Before you go, sir. Do we have a Bombardier in the area?"

"As far as I am aware, the one you flew out in is still there."

"That's one of..." I hesitated.

"I thought you knew. I arranged the flight, remember?"

"It's waiting for me?"

"I thought you might need it, so I told him to hang around a few days to see how things developed."

"You knew about Better Tomorrows?"

"We look after our own, Harry. You know that. When they approached you both we thought we'd have a look. There was nothing immediately obvious, except the smell. I didn't like the smell. I hope you don't feel we were interfering."

I shook my head. "No, sir. I'm glad you were there."

I hung up and looked down at Jean, where she was still sitting on the floor.

"I know you're sick. People like you are incomplete. There's something missing. You look at suffering, even suffering children, and you feel nothing. You don't care. To me that means you're sick. As though you had grown with only one leg and one arm, or a kidney missing. Only what's missing is your humanity."

"Spare me the—"

"Don't. I still might shoot you. I don't expect you to understand. I'm just telling you, if you strike a deal and help the Feds or the CIA, keep your nose clean. Because if I ever come across you again. I will kill you."

She didn't answer, and a couple of minutes later the colonel arrived with his men.

TWENTY-THREE

I HADN'T SHOWERED OR CHANGED MY CLOTHES. I figured I'd do that on the plane.

It was four in the morning when we touched down in New Jersey. I had showered and slept, but I had no clothes to change into, so when I came down the steps of the Bombardier Global 8000, I still looked like an extra from a zombie movie. Fortunately the brigadier was at the bottom of those steps with his Bentley. He ushered me into the back and we moved off into the predawn, toward Manhattan.

We drove in silence for a while as I tried to organize my thoughts. Eventually he looked at me and said, "You need time to think."

I nodded, then sighed and shrugged. "How much can you think? There are two or three facts."

"Then there is how you feel about those facts."

"Sure, but we both know, sir, that you have to disconnect from how you feel. Where other people are concerned, you have to be objective."

He gave a small, wry laugh and we both watched as the mighty Hudson slipped by beneath us.

"I know," I said. "Nobody can be objective, especially where other people are concerned. But that's philosophy. In real life we know what we have to do, and it's not always the same as what we want to do."

He nodded. "You know, whatever you decide, we'll support you."

"That means a lot."

"But if you'll allow me, I'd like to give you my opinion."

"I'd appreciate it."

"This is a conversation you should be having with Claire, and it's a decision you should take together."

I didn't answer for a long while. It was as we were approaching my brownstone on East 128th that I finally said, "How long will it be, sir, after what she has been through, before she can be objective and make a smart choice, or a smart decision?"

The Bentley pulled up outside my house. He reached in his coat pocket and pulled out a ticket and a renewal of the passport I had lost somewhere in Africa.

"Your flight to Jackson departs at eleven AM. From Teterboro. You should get three around three PM. I've hired you a car. Grab four hours' sleep, shower and change your clothes, and go and talk to Claire. Perhaps she will never be able to make an objective, sensible choice with regard to what has happened. But that's because she is human, Harry. And we humans are quintessentially subjective and illogical. You'll just have to go and see what happens. Try and work it out."

———

IT WAS after four PM when I finally rolled into Pinedale in the Ranger the Brigadier had hired for me. I crossed the river and with a strange feeling of nausea and excitement I turned into North Franklin and made a right into Magnolia, where I parked outside Claire's house.

I sat for a long moment, more terrified than I ever was by a gun or a knife. Finally I opened the door and made my way across the lawn to the front door. I rang the bell and heard the bell chime inside. I was overcome by a strange sense of déjà vu. I heard steps inside and felt sick.

The door opened and she was standing there, as she had been that other time, in jeans and a Snoopy sweatshirt, with no makeup on and her hair in a ponytail. But this time she had blue bags under her eyes. She looked pale and drawn. Her eyes widened in astonishment and I thought I saw joy there too. Then she frowned a professional kind of frown and reached up to touch the bruises on my face. Her eyes clouded as the memories came back of how I had got them. She said softly, "Harry."

"I'm sorry," I said. "I should have called. There just never seemed a moment. I came as fast as I could. I can't remember when I wasn't on a plane."

She smiled. It was a sad smile. "That other time you called at my door your face was also bruised. I asked you what had happened."

I smiled too. "I think I told you I'd used it to bruise some knuckles."

"Don't stand there on the doorstep. You'd better come in."

I followed her to the living room. She sat on the sofa and for a moment I remained standing. She said, "I didn't know then what your life was like."

I sat carefully on one of the armchairs. "I didn't know, Claire. I thought it was all over. I resigned. I wanted us to make a new life together."

She met my eye and held it. There were tears in hers. "I know, Harry. I know that. But it's something you can't control, isn't it."

I drew breath to say I could, but ended up saying, "I don't know. There is nobody left, nobody I know of."

We sat in silence, looking at each other while she wept silently. Eventually she spoke with difficulty, her voice catching in her throat.

"I could never go through that again, Harry. I know I owe you my life, I can only imagine what you must have gone through to save me, and I realize that is the measure of how much you care..."

She trailed off. I said, quietly, "But—"

She shook her head, staring up at the ceiling, "I just, I couldn't... Maybe in a month, a few weeks. I don't know. I have these terrible dreams. I am terrified all the time. I long to have you here, beside me, but then I remember."

I left my chair and knelt in front of her, holding her hands in mine. I kissed her.

"Take your time. Recover. Heal. If you need to forget me, do that. But Claire, always remember that whatever you need, anything at all, I will be here for you. All you need to do is call."

I stood. She didn't let go of my hands. "Are you leaving? Do you want to stay the night?"

I hesitated, then shook my head. "When you're ready, when you know for sure, call me."

She didn't see me to the door. I crossed the lawn and climbed behind the wheel of the Ranger. I fired her up and pulled away. I didn't know where I was going. Probably to hell. If that was where the Devil was, I was going to find him.

Don't miss BLOODY RETRIBUTION. The riveting sequel in the Harry Bauer Thriller series.

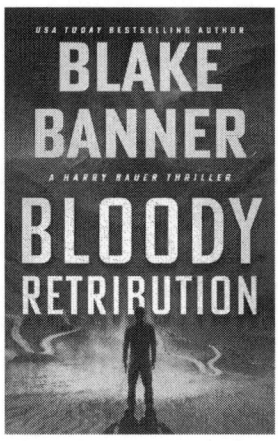

Scan the QR code below to purchase BLOODY RETRIBUTION.

Or go to: righthouse.com/bloody-retribution

NOTE: flip to the very end to read an exclusive sneak peak...

DON'T MISS ANYTHING!

If you want to stay up to date on all new releases in this series, with this author, or with any of our new deals, you can do so by joining our newsletters below.

In addition, you will immediately gain access to our entire *Right House VIP Library,* which includes many riveting Mystery and Thriller novels for your enjoyment!

righthouse.com/email

(Easy to unsubscribe. No spam. Ever.)

ALSO BY BLAKE BANNER

Up to date books can be found at:
www.righthouse.com/blake-banner

ROGUE THRILLERS
Gates of Hell (Book 1)
Hell's Fury (Book 2)

ALEX MASON THRILLERS
Odin (Book 1)
Ice Cold Spy (Book 2)
Mason's Law (Book 3)
Assets and Liabilities (Book 4)
Russian Roulette (Book 5)
Executive Order (Book 6)
Dead Man Talking (Book 7)
All The King's Men (Book 8)
Flashpoint (Book 9)
Brotherhood of the Goat (Book 10)
Dead Hot (Book 11)
Blood on Megiddo (Book 12)
Son of Hell (Book 13)

HARRY BAUER THRILLER SERIES
Dead of Night (Book 1)
Dying Breath (Book 2)
The Einstaat Brief (Book 3)
Quantum Kill (Book 4)
Immortal Hate (Book 5)
The Silent Blade (Book 6)
LA: Wild Justice (Book 7)

Breath of Hell (Book 8)
Invisible Evil (Book 9)
The Shadow of Ukupacha (Book 10)
Sweet Razor Cut (Book 11)
Blood of the Innocent (Book 12)
Blood on Balthazar (Book 13)
Simple Kill (Book 14)
Riding The Devil (Book 15)
The Unavenged (Book 16)
The Devil's Vengeance (Book 17)
Bloody Retribution (Book 18)
Rogue Kill (Book 19)
Blood for Blood (Book 20)

DEAD COLD MYSTERY SERIES
An Ace and a Pair (Book 1)
Two Bare Arms (Book 2)
Garden of the Damned (Book 3)
Let Us Prey (Book 4)
The Sins of the Father (Book 5)
Strange and Sinister Path (Book 6)
The Heart to Kill (Book 7)
Unnatural Murder (Book 8)
Fire from Heaven (Book 9)
To Kill Upon A Kiss (Book 10)
Murder Most Scottish (Book 11)
The Butcher of Whitechapel (Book 12)
Little Dead Riding Hood (Book 13)
Trick or Treat (Book 14)
Blood Into Wine (Book 15)
Jack In The Box (Book 16)
The Fall Moon (Book 17)
Blood In Babylon (Book 18)
Death In Dexter (Book 19)
Mustang Sally (Book 20)

A Christmas Killing (Book 21)
Mommy's Little Killer (Book 22)
Bleed Out (Book 23)
Dead and Buried (Book 24)
In Hot Blood (Book 25)
Fallen Angels (Book 26)
Knife Edge (Book 27)
Along Came A Spider (Book 28)
Cold Blood (Book 29)
Curtain Call (Book 30)

THE OMEGA SERIES
Dawn of the Hunter (Book 1)
Double Edged Blade (Book 2)
The Storm (Book 3)
The Hand of War (Book 4)
A Harvest of Blood (Book 5)
To Rule in Hell (Book 6)
Kill: One (Book 7)
Powder Burn (Book 8)
Kill: Two (Book 9)
Unleashed (Book 10)
The Omicron Kill (Book 11)
9mm Justice (Book 12)
Kill: Four (Book 13)
Death In Freedom (Book 14)
Endgame (Book 15)

ABOUT US

Right House is an independent publisher created by authors for readers. We specialize in Action, Thriller, Mystery, and Crime novels.

If you enjoyed this novel, then there is a good chance you will like what else we have to offer! Please stay up to date by using any of the links below.

Join our mailing lists to stay up to date -->
righthouse.com/email
Visit our website --> righthouse.com
Contact us --> contact@righthouse.com

 facebook.com/righthousebooks
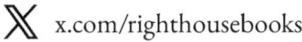 x.com/righthousebooks
 instagram.com/righthousebooks

EXCLUSIVE SNEAK PEAK OF...

BLOODY RETRIBUTION

CHAPTER 1

I was up at the bar at Carlow East, looking down at a pint of Guinness and a shot of Bushmills chaser. It was three in the morning. I was feeling sorry for myself, and the Irish guy who was wiping down the bar wasn't helping. Barmen should be like therapists. They should listen, not talk, and they should make empathetic faces and noises. This guy didn't get it.

"Sure, and didn't I get home and find her in our matrimonial bed with my own brother? And didn't she run home to her feckin' mother and blame me for neglecting her? While me own brother sits and quotes feckin' Milton at me. An English poet, for Christ's sake. 'Sean,' he says, 'It's all about perspective,' he says. 'The mind is its own place, and can make a heaven of hell, and a hell of heaven. So if I was you,' he says, pullin' on his feckin' pants, 'I'd reframe this whole thing in your mind. After all, wasn't I doin' you a favor, after all?'"

My cell rang, and I watched him as I pulled it from my pocket. He was saying, "I mean, it was fifteen of the best years of me life spent behind bars, but I don't regret a bit of it."

I said, "Yeah?"

It was the brigadier. "Harry, where are you?"

"I'm at Carlow East, on Lexington, drowning my sorrows."

"Are you drunk?"

"I keep trying, but I don't seem to be making it."

"I'll be there in five minutes."

"Is the colonel with you?"

There was a short pause, then, "You are drunk, Harry."

I sighed. "Okay, see you in five."

The colonel, Jane Harrison, right then, after two Guinness and four shots, was the only woman in the world capable of understanding me and making me happy. And it was down to me to cut through the crap and make her see that.

Maybe Sean was right. The mind was its own place and could make a hell of heaven. I took a good pull on the Guinness and chased it down with the shot. My mind had just turned to Claire, in Pinedale, and I was considering that she was also the only woman in the world capable of understanding me and making me happy, and it was down to me to cut through the crap and make her see that, when the brigadier climbed on the stool next to me and told Sean, "I'll have what he's having and give him another shot, would you?"

We took our drinks to a table, and he sat opposite me. I noticed there was rain on the shoulders of his coat.

"I have a job for you."

"I told you I hadn't made up my mind yet."

He gave a brief nod. He had gray eyes, and they were cold right then. It was an expression I had seen in him before, just before he shot somebody.

"Well," he said, without much feeling, "you can either make up your mind now or just do the job and make up your mind afterwards."

I blinked at him. He gave a small sigh.

"You know, Harry, perhaps you were misinformed on your way here. Life is shit, and it only gets worse. You have one major problem in life. Women want to sleep with you, but they don't want to marry you."

I felt a jolt of anger in my belly and muttered, "Thanks!"

He shook his head. "Don't think I am making little of it. I happen to know what that's like. But here's a couple of thoughts for you. One, it's better than it being the other way around…"

He paused for me to think about that, and I couldn't help smiling. "Fair point, sir."

"And you get more of what you focus on. So the longer you sit around feeling sorry for yourself, the worse the situation will become." He pointed at my drinks. "And keep this up much longer and they won't even want to sleep with you anymore." He raised his shot. "Cheers!"

We toasted and knocked them back. He put down the glass and leaned forward.

"The best way to shake these blues you're wallowing in is to see face to face just how hard it can get for people worse off than you."

I grunted. "Where?"

"At a lithium mine in Argentina, in the foothills of the Andes."

I frowned. "Who's down there?"

He sat back and took a deep breath, like he was thinking. "Well, that is sort of the point. We're not sure. We have reports that the mine is using slave labor. The reports are not reliable – at least, we are not sure whether they are reliable or not. If they are, then men, women, and children are being exploited as slaves in the mine and the processing plants."

"So this is not a hit. You want me to investigate."

"Initially, yes. If you find the reports are accurate, then you would identify the target or targets and execute the hits. We would also want you to shut down the mine."

"Shut it down?"

He raised an eyebrow. "Yes. We'd like to make it unattractive as an investment so that our own investors can move in and take it over."

I had no idea what a lithium mine would look like, or how you'd shut it down, but I could see the kids, half naked, hungry, probably beaten, and without thinking, I said, "Okay, have you made the arrangements? When do I go?"

"As soon as possible. You'll be a travel writer exploring Argentina and the Argentine Andes. That will give you some cover and a reason to snoop around. But be cautious because my guess is that security will be tight. The consequences for them if they are caught could be very severe. They'll be protecting themselves."

"So I just turn up and start asking questions about what the town has to offer...?"

"No, we've attached you to the magazine *Vagabond*. You will in essence be working for them, and we have asked them to approach the mayor of the village."

"What village?"

"Poman. It's about ninety miles from the nearest large town, Catamarca – thirty miles as the crow flies, but three times that climbing into the foothills of the Andes. So the approach we have made to the mayor is that you are writing about the Argentine Andes, and it might draw some tourism. We imagine that he will be courteous and accommodating but encourage you to explore farther north or farther south. You should at least have a week or two in which to investigate the mine."

"Where is the mine in relation to the village?"

"Three miles north. The exact coordinates will be in your file. The main access is from Highway 46, which lies about two miles to the east. However, that access will take you to a large barbed wire gate and fence protected by armed guards."

"I won't be going in that way."

"Your best approach is by night along a broad dirt track that leads from the village to a rear entrance. This is the route used by the villagers who work at the mine. Aside from that, I can tell you little. We have no intelligence regarding alarm systems, security, dogs..." He trailed off, shaking his head, then added, "This is why your mission is initially primarily reconnaissance."

"Okay, will I have any contact there?"

"I will be at Catamarca. I'll be staying at the American. When you need to report, you meet me there, and we will discuss the action to be taken. We have access to some ordnance in Argentina."

"I don't know what a lithium mine looks like. I don't know what I'll need to shut it down."

"You'll find that information in your brief. If that proves necessary, we will provide you with the hardware. Right now, what you need to focus on is whether there is in fact slavery going on there. If the answer to that is in the positive, then we need to know how bad it is. Is there torture involved? If so, who is being tortured, and how? Are people being murdered? In what numbers and again, how? Once we have these facts nailed down, we can start thinking about the steps to be taken."

"Okay." I nodded. "I'm in." And as I said it, I realized that it felt good.

———

THE FLIGHT from New York to Buenos Aires was over five thousand miles, and from there, I had to take another flight in an old prop-driven Fokker five hundred miles across Argentina into the foothills of the Andes. We finally touched down in Catamarca in the early afternoon. I collected my large rucksack, slung it in the back of my RAM 1500 rental, and set off along the imaginatively named Acceso al Aeropuerto toward their Highway 38, which would lead me, eventually, through the mountains up to the village of Poman.

The road was long and straight and ran through the center of a flat, featureless valley populated by low, scrubby trees I could not identify. The earth was a rusty red, and here and there, vast, circular fields had been plowed out: gigantic scars where the cycle of life had been industrialized to feed the human plague and the insatiable numbered accounts of the fattest, greediest parasites.

To my right, the Andes rose suddenly, a massive, dark blue

wall against the near-white sky. After fifteen minutes, I came to an intersection with a blue sign that told me this was Route 19, which lead me straight toward the mountains. Slowly and steadily, I began to climb as the sun slipped into bronzed afternoon and the shadows around me began to grow and stretch.

I climbed steadily through deep gorges and canyons where the steep sides of the hills crowded in over the road. The bends were tight hairpins, and the road was narrow, meaning every bend was also blind and forced me to go slowly, even though the traffic was minimal.

My GPS told me it would be a two-hour drive, but by the time I finally came out onto the arid highlands, an hour and three quarters had passed since I'd pulled out of the airport. Here at least the road was long and straight. I put my foot down and hurtled through the high desert closing on a hundred miles per hour. It was a landscape of desolation where what few trees there were had become gnarled by the summer heat and the frigid nights and winters.

Suddenly, as though I had driven through some quantum portal, the desolate desert threw up an orchard, and then another. I slowed. A garden appeared and a shaded path among old, Spanish houses with terracotta roofs and orange groves. Then, just as suddenly, I was entering a village with grim, narrow streets, dark houses with no windows, that had once been painted white, yellow, or salmon pink with lime wash but now were colored only with grime and neglect.

I slowed practically to a walking pace moving over the broken asphalt, among the cracked sidewalks and the dilapidated houses until I came to Jerónimo Luís de Cabrera Street. There, on my right, opposite the volunteer fire truck station, was a building that had probably been beige in the 1790s. It had stucco that had been picked out in white, probably around the same time, and a big hand-painted sign stuck to the wall claiming that the Pomanti Hotel had bedrooms, Wi-Fi, private bathrooms, and a thing called a yakuzi, which I guessed was not a Latin plural for a member of the Japanese underworld.

There were four doors. They were all painted yellow and white, and they were all closed. I parked the car in an area of wasteland just past the hostel, killed the engine, and walked to the middle door. It had seven flags hanging above it. None of them was the Stars and Stripes, and the only European one was Spanish. There was no bell, so I rapped with my knuckles and pushed.

The door juddered and swung open onto a small entrance hall with a gray tiled floor and a large arch onto an internal patio. There were a couple of wooden-framed armchairs that were modern and fashionable about the same time the Beatles had pudding basin haircuts, and there were a couple of dark, wooden doors, one on my right and one on my left. They had glass panels in them, but the one on my right had a printed sign stuck to the glass with sticking tape. It read *Oficina*. I took a wild guess and figured that meant office. So I stepped inside, knocked, and pushed through the door. There were two women there behind a melamine reception desk. One looked old enough to be Methuselah's grandmother. She had one tooth left in her lower jaw, and that looked even older than she did.

The other woman was in her early twenties and might have been the model for the clichéd Hollywood Latina, complete with black eyes and a sultry scowl. They were both staring at me. Mama Methuselah had her mouth sagging slightly, and her one tooth seemed to be pointing at me, like some weird kind of dowsing rod designed to seek out Americans. The other one had her head tilted forward and was giving me the treatment from under perfect eyebrows.

I smiled, but nothing happened. Sultry and ancient was the tone, and nothing was going to change that. "Habla ingles?"

Sultry said, "You are in Argentina. In Argentina, people espeakin' espanish."

"If I promise to learn, will you check my booking and show me my room?"

She sighed. "What is your name?"

"Bauer, Harry Bauer. I have a reservation."

She looked at a flat screen behind the desk and rattled at the keys on her keyboard. The action looked weirdly out of place in the setting. While she rattled, I looked up at the ceiling. It was exquisitely made of wooden beams that were probably more than two hundred years old.

"You are writer."

Something in her tone made me look at her. It wasn't a question. It was a bald statement, but I said, "Yes."

"I take you to your room."

"Thanks."

She came around the desk on shapely legs that made her hips swing, and I followed those legs and those hips across an internal patio with potted palms and up a wooden staircase to a galleried landing with evenly spaced heavy wooden doors in a white lime-washed wall. At the end, she unlocked one of those doors and went in ahead of me. I followed down a short passage. The floor was tiled in terracotta. There was a bathroom on my right, and then the room opened out. There was a big brass bed, and as I dumped my bag on it, she opened a set of tall, green, slatted French doors onto a small balcony that overlooked the ugly street below. Over the bed, there was a large, wooden fan like a propeller.

She stood framed in the open terrace door. The contrast made it hard to see the expression on her face. "What you are writing?"

"I'm a travel writer. I write about interesting, remote places."

"There is nothing interesting in Poman."

I gave my shoulders a small shrug. "Maybe there is and you just don't know about it."

"How long you are going to stay?"

"I don't know. If you are right and there is nothing interesting here, I'll leave in a week. If you're wrong, I'll stay longer."

She didn't move. She didn't react. After a moment, she said, "What is interesting?"

I crossed my arms and raised my shoulders high, like her question made thought, and therefore a bigger shrug, necessary.

"I don't know: music festivals, traditional carnivals, archeological remains..." I trailed off. "Most places have something. You're in the foothills of the Andes. That's interesting."

"There are no music festivals here, no carnival, no archeology."

I felt like telling her the woman downstairs with the tooth was an interesting archeological relic but pulled out my wallet instead and held out ten bucks.

"Thanks," I said. "If you think of anything that might be interesting for an American writer, let me know."

"We are all American, Mr. Bauer. You are North American, I am South American, but we are all American."

"Yeah," I said, "I know" and smiled on the side of my face where it doesn't look like a smile. She approached, took the ten North American dollars, brushed past me, and opened the door. "Oh," I said and stopped her. "I'm expecting a telephone call from your mayor. He thinks Poman is real interesting."

She waited for me to finish, with her eyes fixed on the terracotta tiles at her feet. When I was done, she left, closing the door behind her.

CHAPTER 2

I SHOWERED AND SHAVED, AND BY THE TIME I WAS putting on a clean shirt, there was a tap at the door. When I opened it, Sultry was there leaning with her ass against the gallery balustrade.

"The mayor's office on the telephone for you."

I arched an eyebrow at her. "Can't you put it through to my room?"

"Is no workin' the telephone in your room."

"Right."

"They fixin' it."

By which I figured she meant they were fixing the bug. I nodded. "What's your name?"

"Carla Montoya."

She led me down to reception again where the tame zombie was still pointing at me with her gravestone tooth. I picked up the old bakelite receiver and said, "Hello? This is Harry Bauer."

I was surprised to hear a woman's voice on the other end. Contrary to what Colonel Jane Harris, the chef of operations at Odin believes, I am not a misogynist. I believe women are eminently well suited to any job that involves telling people what to do. I just don't expect them to be in those jobs in the foothills of the Andes.

And it turned out I was right. The pretty voice said, "Mr. Bauer, I am telephoning you on behalf of Mr. Nelson McCormack, the mayor of Poman. His English is not so good, but he would like to invite you to have luncheon with him, if you are free."

I smiled at the menacing tooth across the reception desk, and the bulging eyes that lay staring behind it. "That would be wonderful," I said.

"Will you be free in half an hour?"

"As soon as you like."

There was a smile in the voice when she said, "I'll be there in ten minutes."

I hung up and turned. Carla was leaning on the jamb of the open door, watching me. There were a lot of dark emotions swimming in her dark brown eyes, but the one that was most evident on the surface was judgment, judgment and her sister, condemnation. I smiled without feeling.

"Did something interesting just happen in Poman?"

Her lip curled, and she pushed off the jamb. "If something interesting happen in Poman, you don't see it and you don't hear it. It happen in the dark, at night."

I was torn between boredom and curiosity. So I made for the door, then paused and frowned. By that time, she was behind the desk, leaning on it with her elbows.

"Americans!" She said it like she was summing up everything that was wrong with fast food. "Makin' bombs, invisible airplanes, laser guns, everything to fight the Chinese and the Russians. Meantime the Chinese is investing, investing, investing, buying all the poor countries in the world. One belt, one road, and stupid America just watching, arguing about men in women's toilets and sports, while China becomin' bigger, more rich, more powerful."

I stared at her for a long moment, then gave my head a twitch.

"You don't make Poman sound boring. You make it sound interesting."

She crooked her index finger and rapped it on the counter. "Why America don't invest here? Make a partnership with Argentina! Build a factory for light! One F16 can make that factory and bring light and water to thousands of people!"

I returned to the desk and leaned on it, looking down at her. "Isn't that your government's job?"

"But they do nothing! They just give license the Chinese government. And they invest their money, no in makin' light; they invest their money in darkness. Things that happen at night, when doors and windows are closed and nobody is lookin'!"

I made a face of ironic disbelief and said, "Yeah, right. No music festivals, but a Fu Manchu conspiracy?"

I was about to return to my room and tell her to call me when the car arrived when there was a honk outside. A moment later, her cell pinged, and she gave me a look that said she'd like to skin me alive and eat my heart raw.

"Your paymaster is here, in the car outside."

I made a show of indignation and scowled at her. "I don't have a paymaster, sweetheart. I am freelance, independent. I work for me."

At the door, I stopped and turned back. "You have something to tell me, tell me. Cut out the snide comments and talk."

Outside, the midday sun was hot. The temperature was probably only in the nineties, but at that altitude, in the thin air, ninety can feel like a hundred and ten.

There was a Mercedes Maybach blocking the road outside and an attractive, well-dressed woman leaning against the passenger door watching me as I came out. She smiled and approached with her hand held out.

"Mr. Bauer? I am Rosario Fuentes, assistant to the mayor, Don Nelson McCormack. He has asked me to take you to Nacho's for a drink, and he will meet us there very soon."

I told her it sounded good, and she opened the door for me.

The smile we exchanged was perhaps a little friendlier than the occasion called for.

It was a short drive through dilapidated orchards and lots where half the houses seemed to be half built. The rule seemed to be half of the ground floor was finished, and the rest of the house was raw cement and concrete with gaping holes where the windows should be.

I told her, "I guess there was a property boom that didn't last long enough for the building boom that followed to get finished?"

She smiled. For a moment, I thought she wasn't going to answer, but then she said, "Economies in rural Argentina are very fragile. People do what they can. When times are good, they invest in their property. Sometimes the money runs out."

"It looks that way. What about you? Are you from Poman?"

Again the protracted silence, like she was calibrating her answer.

"My parents were from Poman. My father was the doctor. He did not agree with the idea of investing in property." She glanced at me. "He said there are many kinds of property. A prison is a property. Better to invest in a good lawyer than make your prison more comfortable."

"Smart guy. So what did he do? He sent you to college to study law in Catamarca?"

The contraction on her face was almost imperceptible. "He sent me to study law in Buenos Aires."

"How old were you?"

She looked like she didn't know whether to be affronted or simply surprised. Instead of making up her mind, she said, "We are here."

We pulled in to a crescent drive off the road. The building was modern – or had been in the '50s – rectilinear white boxes stacked on top of each other, with lots of plate glass. Outside, there were tables made of steel tubing and plastic with their corresponding chairs. She killed the engine, and we climbed out.

Before we got to the door, a guy I took to be the owner came stumbling out, reaching for her with both hands and grinning too hard. As he drew closer, he didn't touch her. Her face said that wasn't allowed. Instead, he gestured toward the door and bowed. He kept saying, "Doña Rosario" and mumbling in Spanish.

She ignored him, and I followed her inside. There was a small dining room with a dozen tables made of melamine and steel tubing and a bar that ran down the right hand side. Rosario crossed the room and pushed through a door that said PRIVADO. I followed. The swing of her hips made that easy. She pushed through a second door, and we were out on a flagged patio with an exotic garden and a fountain that made a good pretence of being ancient and possibly Greek.

There were two steel tubing tables that had been pushed together and covered in a white linen tablecloth. They were set with the restaurant's best stainless steel and lead-free crystal.

She took a seat with her back to the yard and the fountain, and I sat opposite her. The door opened, and the owner came out, still bowing. She rattled something at him in Spanish. I head something about martini, and then she looked a question at me. I said, "Scotch, on the rocks."

When he'd gone, I said, "I hope my question didn't offend you."

She shrugged and forced a smile. "Why should it offend me?"

I returned the smile. "I can't imagine." I gestured at her with an open hand. "You are obviously a very elegant, sophisticated, cultured woman. That doesn't happen in four or five years of college while you're burning the midnight oil trying to memorize contract law."

She arched a very elegant eyebrow. "Wow."

I raised my shoulders an eighth of an inch. "The magazine pays me a lot because I am very observant."

"Papa sent me to a private boarding school in Buenos Aires, then I went to university there."

I grinned. "I could have told you that. What I am wondering is how the mayor of Poman can afford you."

"You are becoming impertinent, Mr. Bauer." She said it like she didn't really mind.

"I'm here looking for what's interesting. Right now, the most interesting thing I have found in Poman is you. And I am wondering why the mayor of a tiny village in the foothills of the Andes, where the hotel hasn't even got a bar, has an assistant with a degree in law from the best university in Argentina and enough style and intelligence to be on the board of any of Argentina's multinationals."

She was quiet for a long moment, trying to read my face. Finally she said, "How do you know I have a degree in law?"

"It's written on your forehead and in the way you walk. I'd go so far as to say you did a masters at an American university. You walk like a United States defense attorney. But I might be wrong, and then I'd lose my reputation and my credibility."

She blinked slowly three times before saying, "Columbia. If I didn't know it was impossible, I'd say you'd been checking up on me."

I gave a small laugh. "But then I'd know the answer to my question, wouldn't I? I am just good at guessing. Let's face it, what's a girl like you doing in a place like this?"

The door opened, and a waiter stepped out with a tray bearing a martini and a Scotch on the rocks. When he'd gone, we toasted and she sipped. As she set down her glass, she said, "The mayor of Poman is my uncle. This is a very small town, and most people are related. A year ago, the LitArg corporation was founded for the purpose of finding and exploiting lithium mines in South America. They believe this is the oil of tomorrow, and Argentina will be the Saudi Arabia of the future."

"Makes sense, but how does that affect you?"

"The LitArg prospectors found a very large lithium mine outside Poman, and my uncle found he was out of his depth negotiating with these high-powered lawyers. So he asked me to come and help." She gave a small shrug. "In Argentina, family counts."

I made an appreciative face. "So that's good news for Poman, right?"

She didn't answer. She just sipped her drink. Maybe she thought the question was rhetorical. So I added, "Well, I am extremely flattered that your uncle dragged you away from your meetings with LitArg to entertain me, a humble hack from a travel rag."

"How many meetings do you think we have a month, Mr. Bauer? Once the contracts are settled, there is very little contact, as you well know. In fact, I will be going back to Buenos Aires in another week or so. I am sure you are also aware that for my uncle, a visit from a journalist representing a magazine – not a rag, as you say – such as *Vagabond*, which is read all over the world, could be an important boost for tourism. Are all travel journalists as suspicious as you, Mr. Bauer?"

I laughed. "I am not suspicious, Rosario, and please call me Harry. Maybe I am just flirting with you. Are you married?"

"My goodness! You don't waste time, do you?"

"Apparently I only have a week."

She gave a small sigh. "I am married, Mr. Bauer – Harry – to my job and to my family."

"Package deal, huh?"

"That is the way it is in Latin America. Do you think this is an appropriate conversation for"—she gestured at me with an open hand—"a journalist and a representative of local government?"

I smiled. "Not really, Rosario. But as you said, I am a journalist, and journalists are not supposed to be appropriate. We are the fourth estate. It's our job to be inappropriate."

Her face said she was feeling skeptical. "The fourth estate? Before the French revolution, in France, the church was the first estate, the aristocracy was the second, and the commoners were the third. Then the printing press came along, and problematic thinkers and idealists started printing leaflets, spreading seditious ideas. It was Edmund Burk who called you the fourth estate, and if I am not mistaken, he was mocking you."

I arched an eyebrow at her over my whiskey. "Just because I mockingly call you the desirable lady across the table, it doesn't mean you are *not* the desirable lady across the table."

She didn't smile, but her cheeks did color. "Please, Mr. Bauer, you have to stop this."

There were voices outside. The door opened, and a small crowd of men spilled through. At a quick estimate, I calculated there were about twice as many as would fit at the table. The one at the center was in his late sixties in an expensive off-the-peg suit. His hair and his skin said he'd spent a lot of hours recently in a hair salon and a beauty parlor having the last sixty years of toiling in unforgiving Andean fields cleaned out of his skin and his hair with expensive lotions and massages. He probably didn't know where Paris was, but he knew that was where his lotions came from.

I stood.

Two guys went and stood on the other side of the door. Two stood on this side of the door, and two more went and stood out in the yard. The sixty-plus guy in the expensive suit and hair grinned and held out his hand. "Señor Bauer," he said with a little sing-song. "Es un gran placer darle la bienvenida a este, nuestro humilde pueblo."

He glanced at Rosario as I took his hand and shook it.

"Mr. Nelson McCormack says it is his pleasure to welcome you to this, our humble village."

I gave his hand a good squeeze. "Please tell him it is an honor for me to be here." She translated, and I added, "So far I have found it fascinating and surprising, and I am anxious to discover everything there is to know about it."

He nodded and listened as she translated, with his mouth slightly open. Then he grinned at me and nodded more vigorously. We all sat, and he started giving elaborate instructions to the waiter.

Scan the QR code below to purchase BLOODY RETRIBUTION.
Or go to: righthouse.com/bloody-retribution

Made in United States
Orlando, FL
02 January 2026

76166240R10120